"The coroner says someone hit your father in the back of the head and probably knocked him out."

"So they snuck up on him."

"Or he trusted the person enough to turn his back."

"That makes me feel even worse." She looked up at the ceiling, willing the tears not to fall. Her eyes and head ached from crying. "Though why it's easier for me to think he was killed by someone he hated than someone he liked—I mean, he's still gone, either way."

"I'm sorry," Chris said.

"That helps a little," she said. "Knowing other people hate that this happened and that some of them will miss him, too."

Chris stood. "I'd better go. But just remember—you and I are on the same side. We both want to find out the truth about what happened to your father."

She nodded. "Finding out who did this won't bring Dad back, but not knowing just adds to the loss. Does that make sense?"

"It makes a lot of sense." He rested his hand on her shoulder. The touch was brief but reassuring. She felt its warmth long after he had left her alone in the kitchen.

CONSPIRACY IN THE ROCKIES

CINDI MYERS

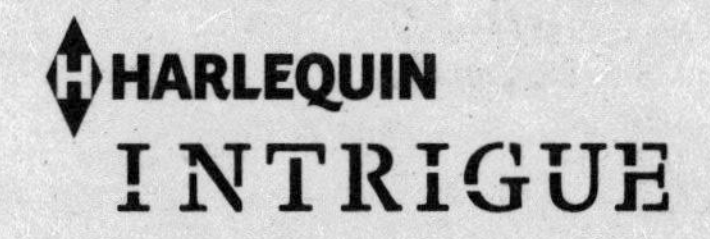

To Winston and Lucy.

Recycling programs for this product may not exist in your area.

ISBN-13: 978-1-335-48938-8

Conspiracy in the Rockies

This edition published by arrangement with Harlequin Books S.A.

For questions and comments about the quality of this book, please contact us at CustomerService@Harlequin.com.

Harlequin Enterprises ULC
22 Adelaide St. West, 41st Floor
Toronto, Ontario M5H 4E3, Canada
www.Harlequin.com

Printed in U.S.A.

Cindi Myers is the author of more than fifty novels. When she's not plotting new romance story lines, she enjoys skiing, gardening, cooking, crafting and daydreaming. A lover of small-town life, she lives with her husband and two spoiled dogs in the Colorado mountains.

Books by Cindi Myers

Harlequin Intrigue

Eagle Mountain: Search for Suspects

Disappearance at Dakota Ridge
Conspiracy in the Rockies

The Ranger Brigade: Rocky Mountain Manhunt

Investigation in Black Canyon
Mountain of Evidence
Mountain Investigation
Presumed Deadly

Eagle Mountain Murder Mystery: Winter Storm Wedding

Ice Cold Killer
Snowbound Suspicion
Cold Conspiracy
Snowblind Justice

Eagle Mountain Murder Mystery

Saved by the Sheriff
Avalanche of Trouble
Deputy Defender
Danger on Dakota Ridge

Visit the Author Profile page at Harlequin.com.

CAST OF CHARACTERS

Willow Russell—A job loss has forced Willow back to the family ranch, where she clashes with her father, Sam. But Sam's murder pushes her into the role of both victim and suspect.

Deputy Chris Delray—He's the official water cop—charged with enforcing the state's complicated water laws among the network of ranches that utilize public irrigation ditches. When he finds Sam Russell's body in one of the ditches, he turns his focus to catching a murderer.

Sam Russell—The rancher has lived in Rayford County long enough to make plenty of friends, and a few enemies. The discoveries made after he's murdered point to far too many suspects.

Darla Russell—Sam's ex-wife expects to gain control of the vast Russell Ranch after Sam's death.

Emmett Caspar—Sam's stepson claims he's due to inherit half the ranch.

Von King—The ex-con ranch hand claims to be the only thing keeping the ranch going now that Sam is gone.

Trey Allerton—This handsome veteran leased sixty acres from Sam Russell for a youth ranch, but has yet to make much progress with the project. Upon Sam's death, Trey's rent payments drop to one dollar a year.

Chapter One

The man lay facedown in the ditch, green water flowing over and around him, his gray hair flowing out from his head like a mantle of weeds. His hat, a tan felt Stetson, was caught in a raspberry bush just out of the water, the ripe fruit staining the brim like fresh blood.

"I wanted to pull him out, but I could see he wasn't breathing, and I figured I'd better call you." Perry Webber, the ditch rider for this part of Rayford County, wiped at his hatchet of a nose with a yellow bandanna. "It was a shock, seeing Sam Russell there like that. I've known him over fifteen years. One of the really good guys, solid as a fence post."

Deputy Chris Delray only half listened to Perry's rambling. He studied the body in the ditch and the trampled grass mingled with mud around it. "What time did you find him?" he asked.

Perry pulled out his phone. "It was maybe twenty or twenty-five minutes before I called you, so about ten after seven? I had to run all the way back to my truck, then drive to where I could get a phone signal."

Chris looked around at the cattle pens and crude sheds constructed of rough cedar logs, the wood weathered silver by years in the dry air. A hot breeze sent a dust devil dancing across the empty corrals and bent the tall grass alongside the irrigation ditch. "What brought you out here?" he asked.

"I had to open the number seven gate so Russell could irrigate his south hayfield," Perry said. "Sam called me last night to tell me he wanted to irrigate first thing this morning."

Chris looked down the deep, narrow irrigation ditch that ran parallel to the gravel track where he and Perry had parked. "Where is gate number seven?"

"It's down that way, about a quarter mile." Perry pointed downstream. "I opened it a little after six fifteen, but the water wasn't moving like it should. That usually means a blockage, so I got out my shovel and started walking upstream, looking for whatever was impeding the flow." He stared glumly at the body. "I guess I found it. You reckon his heart gave out or something and he fell in?"

"We'll have to wait for the coroner to find that out," Chris said. He took Perry's arm and steered him away from the ditch and the body. "Did you see anyone else on your way to this spot, or since you arrived here? Any other vehicles pass on the road?"

Perry shook his head. "No." He looked around

them. "I don't see Sam's pickup, either, and we're a ways from the house. How did he get here?"

No sign of a horse or a four-wheeler, either. Chris had never known a rancher to walk when he could ride. He wasn't sure how Sam Russell had died, but he needed to secure the scene to save any evidence that would help them figure that out. "Can you drive until you get a good phone signal and call the sheriff's department?" he asked. "Tell them what happened. I'll stay here with Mr. Russell."

"All right." Perry stuffed the bandanna in his pocket. "But who's going to tell Willow?"

"Who is Willow?" Chris asked.

"She's Sam's daughter. She moved back home a few weeks ago, from somewhere out East, I think."

"Someone from our office will contact her. Don't worry about that now. Just call the sheriff for me."

Perry nodded and headed for the battered red truck parked on the road, Rayford Irrigation District stenciled in fading white letters on the door.

When Perry was gone, Chris took some photos with his phone, placing his steps carefully, alert for any evidence. In the few criminal law classes he'd taken in law school, as well as in the state's law enforcement academy, it had been drilled into him that any unattended death had to be treated as a crime scene until ruled otherwise. Though he had ended up specializing in water law, that information had stuck with him.

The law itself interested him, but after a year spent stuck behind a desk researching every arcane aspect of Colorado's complicated water law for more senior attorneys, he had had enough. He met a sheriff's deputy in eastern Colorado whose job involved enforcing that law and decided that was the job for him. So he'd quit the legal firm, enrolled in the law enforcement academy and here he was, Rayford County's newest deputy and a fully qualified water cop. In four months on the job, he'd gotten to know the officers of the irrigation district and the farmers and ranchers who were the primary members of the district, as well as the five ditch riders who were responsible for managing the water, releasing it for members as they needed it and were entitled to use it. Chris's job was to mediate disputes between members and issue citations to unauthorized users. So far, he'd broken up one fistfight and been shouted at by one angry man, but he never thought he'd have to deal with a dead body.

Just over an hour later, a plume of dust foretold the arrival of another vehicle on the scene. Chris walked out to meet what he hoped was a fellow deputy. But the vehicle that emerged from the dust wasn't a sheriff's department SUV, but a brown late-model F-250, a top-of-the-line King Ranch edition. The vehicle skidded to a stop behind his SUV. The driver's door opened and a woman slid out. She had a braid of black hair that hung past the center of her back and the kind of figure Chris guessed was what people meant by "hourglass"—full breasts and hips and a small waist. He knew he was staring, but had a hard time pulling his gaze away.

"What's going on here?" she called, then started toward him. "Is there some kind of trouble?"

Chris stepped out to intercept her. The last thing he wanted was for her to see the body in the ditch. "I'm Deputy Chris Delray," he said. "Who are you?"

"I'm Willow Russell. My father owns this ranch. Have you seen him?" She pushed her sunglasses up on her head and fixed him with a direct gaze. She had green eyes and olive skin, and lacy dark lashes—a beautiful woman, and a very worried one, from the look of things.

"Why don't we sit over here and talk?" He put a hand on her arm, intending to lead her toward his SUV.

She wrenched out of his grasp. "I'm not going anywhere until you tell me what's going on," she said.

He wasn't going to get away with stalling or lying to her, and he was ashamed of himself for even thinking it. She deserved the truth, even if it was unpleasant. "The ditch rider found your father earlier this morning," he said. "I'm sorry to have to tell you, he's dead."

Her eyes widened and she gasped, then put a hand to her mouth, as if to cover the sound. He hovered, ready to steady her if she looked faint, but she stood firm. She swallowed, then lowered her hand. "What happened?" she asked.

"We don't know yet. I'm waiting for more deputies and the coroner to arrive."

"I want to see him," she said. "Where is he?" She looked around, trying to see past him.

"I don't think you want to do that," he said.

Again that direct gaze. "If it was your father, would you believe he was dead if you didn't see it for yourself? And who better to identify the body than me?" She must have read the hesitation on his face, and pressed her point. "I won't scream or faint," she said. "I'm not that kind of woman."

He nodded. "All right. But you can't touch anything. You can't touch him."

She followed him to the canal and stood beside him, her shoulder almost touching his, staring down at the man in the ditch. Already the body had taken on the stiff appearance of a mannequin. Something not quite human. Her breath hitched, and she put her hand to her mouth again. "That's him," she said, the words muffled.

He gently turned her away. "Let's wait over here for the others to arrive," he said.

He led her back to the trucks, retrieved a bottle of water from the cooler in his back seat and handed it to her. She didn't open it, just held it, looking back toward the ditch, though they could no longer see the body from here. "What do you think happened?" she asked. "Did he have a heart attack or a stroke? He's never sick, but I guess at his age, you never know."

"I don't know," he said. "I'm waiting for help from the sheriff's department. It's better not to touch anything until they get here. Do you know what your father was doing out here this morning?"

She shook her head. "No. He was gone when I got up." A ghost of a smile flickered on her lips, then vanished. "He can't sleep past six and is usually up by five," she said. "But he's always back for breakfast by eight. When he didn't come in, I went out looking for him. He tells me I worry too much, but this time..." She pressed her lips together and looked away, but not before he saw the sheen of tears in her eyes.

The sound of tires on gravel made them both look down the road. Two sheriff's department SUVs parked across from Chris and Willow. A black 4Runner pulled in behind them. The sheriff emerged from the lead SUV. Deputy Jamie Douglas and Deputy Wes Landry got out of the second one. A portly man with a black doctor's bag followed from the 4Runner.

"This is Willow Russell," Chris said. "She's identified the man in the ditch as her father, Samuel Russell."

"I'm very sorry for your loss, Ms. Russell." Sheriff Travis Walker had a solemn maturity that made him seem older than twenty-nine. And he had a reputation as a smart, thorough lawman. "It would be best if you return home to wait while we process the scene. I can send Deputy Douglas with you."

"I'll wait here," Willow said. "I won't get in your way, but I won't leave, either."

Travis paused, then nodded. "All right."

He waited until she had climbed back into the driver's seat of the Ford, then returned to Chris. "What have we got?"

"The ditch rider, Perry Webber, called me at about seven thirty to tell me he'd found rancher Sam Russell's body in the ditch near his loading corrals."

The portly man with the doctor's bag joined them. "Butch Collins," he said to Chris. "County coroner."

Chris nodded. "Deputy Chris Delray."

"Any relation to Ted Delray?" Collins asked.

"My father." Most people in the county knew his dad, one of only a handful of attorneys in the area.

"Wes, you and Jamie wait here," Travis said. "Keep an eye on Ms. Russell." He and Collins followed Chris to the ditch, all of them careful to stand back from the body.

"How long has he been there?" Collins asked. "Anyone know?"

"His daughter says he is usually up between five and six and he wasn't in the house when she came down from her room at seven," Chris said. "Perry found him about ten after seven."

Butch nodded and looked around. "I need a board or something across that ditch so I can examine him before you pull him out."

Travis pried a loose section of fencing from one of the corrals and carried it over to form a bridge over the ditch. The coroner crouched awkwardly over it and began examining the body. Chris looked away, back toward the Ford. Sun glinted off the windshield, making it impossible to see Willow's face, though Jamie stood next to the open driver's-side window, talking.

"Help me turn him over," Butch said. "Easy now."

Chris and Travis knelt in the mud of the ditch bank and eased the dead man on to his back. Chris winced at the gaping wound in Russell's chest, and quickly looked away, his gaze falling on the shotgun beneath the body. "Suicide?" Travis asked.

"I'd say the shotgun blast killed him," Butch said. "Though whether it was self-inflicted or not, I won't know until I get him to the hospital, where I can take a better look." He stood. "Get all the photos and whatever else you need. While you're doing that, I'll call the ambulance to transport him."

"Estimate on the time of death?" Travis asked.

Butch made a face. "You know that as well as I do. He's been there two or three hours, which matches with what the daughter told us."

He walked away. Travis signaled for Wes and Jamie to join them, and they set about photographing and measuring the scene, and combing the surrounding area for evidence. Travis pulled Chris aside. "Let's talk to the daughter," he said.

Chris suspected Willow was watching them as they crossed to the truck. When they stopped beside her, she leveled her same direct gaze. "Well?" she asked.

"What was your father's mood this morning when he left the house?" Travis asked.

"I already told your deputy here that I wasn't awake when Dad left, but I imagine his mood was good," she said. "It usually was."

"Nothing worrying him lately? No concerns about money or his health?"

"No. Why are you asking?"

"Does your father own a shotgun?"

"Yes."

"Do you know where that gun is now?"

"No. Why are you asking this?" Not waiting for the answer, she shoved open the truck door and got out to stand in front of them. "How did my father die?" she asked.

"He was shot in the chest with a shotgun," Travis said.

There was no way to cushion a blow like that. Chris saw the impact of it in the shrinking of her shoulders, and the slight hunching as if she'd taken a hard punch. But she quickly straightened, and inhaled a deep, though shaky breath. "Who shot him?" she asked.

"Do you know someone who would have wanted to do so?" Travis asked. "Did your father have any enemies?"

"Dad has lived in Rayford County for almost seventy years," she said. "There may be people here who don't love him, but I never heard of anyone who hated him."

"Can you think of any reason your father would have taken his own life?" Travis asked.

Another blow, this one blanching the color from her face, but she lifted her chin and held the sheriff's gaze. "No," she said. "My father wouldn't have killed himself. Someone else killed him and you'd better find out who that person is."

Chapter Two

Willow refused the sheriff's offer to have Deputy Douglas drive her back to the ranch, and had declined his suggestion that he call someone to stay with her. "I'd rather be alone right now," she said. "I have a lot of things to think about."

"We may have more questions for you after we get the doctor's report," the sheriff said. She remembered Travis Walker from high school—a tall, good-looking athlete, whom all the girls had crushes on. His reticence made him that much more desirable in their teenage minds. She wasn't as easily impressed these days—looks weren't everything, and she had had her fill of men who wouldn't talk.

"I want to know what the coroner has to say," she said. No tiptoeing around reality with that softer word, *doctor*. "Though my father did not kill himself." She climbed back into the truck and turned the key in the ignition. They stepped back, and let her pass.

She was still replaying the morning's events in her mind a few minutes later when she steered the truck through the gates leading to the ranch house. Before she had even parked, movement by the machine shed across from the house caught her eye. Ranch hand Von King emerged from the shed, a shovel in one hand, a five-gallon bucket in the other. He looked over as she slid out of the truck, and she felt the impact of that gaze.

She didn't like Von—not the hungry way he looked at her when her father wasn't around, or his sullen answers to her attempts to make conversation. She had shared her opinion with her father who, as usual, dismissed her concerns. *Von's all right*, he'd said. *He's a good worker.* That was the highest praise a man like her father could give.

Her impulse was to go inside and avoid Von, but her father's death—his murder, she was sure—didn't give her that luxury. She couldn't be sure Sheriff Walker and his deputies would go out of their way to find out what had happened to her dad, so she would have to do so.

Von looked up at her approach, his eyes hooded, his expression unreadable. Then, when she was almost to him, he grinned. The grin caught her off guard, so different from his usual surly glare. "Willow," he said. No greeting attached, just her name, almost drawled off his tongue, as if he was tasting each letter.

"Have you seen my dad this morning?" she asked.

"Nope."

"He's not in the house and I can't find him anywhere."

"He's probably out on one of the four-wheelers, checking fence or something." He set down the bucket, which she saw now contained a mixture of oil and sand. He plunged the shovel into it, working it up and down. "He likes to do that."

"He's always back by eight for breakfast," she said.

"Before you came home, he'd sometimes stay out all day. Maybe he decided to do that today. I imagine he'll come home when he's ready."

"I'm worried something may have happened to him."

"He's been looking after himself for years."

"Well, I think you should look for him." That would get him out of her sight for a while.

"Can't." He lifted the shovel from the sand and inspected the blade, clean now, with an oily sheen. "Your dad wanted me to clean and sharpen all the hand tools today and he's the boss." *Not you* hung in the air between them, unspoken.

She turned and headed for the house, aware of his gaze burning into her all the way across the yard.

Inside, she switched on the coffeepot to reheat and looked around at the cluttered kitchen, their uneaten breakfast on the table, dirty dishes in the sink. A pair of her father's muddy rubber boots stood by the back door, and a stack of mail was piled on one end of the kitchen counter.

The phone rang and she jumped. The old-fashioned wall-mount phone had a loud bell and a long cord that, when she was a teenager, had allowed her to carry the handset down the hall and lock herself in the bathroom, where she could talk privately, until her father decided she had talked too long. Then he would simply unplug the phone, silencing her conversation. If she objected, he'd say, *Next time, maybe you won't talk so long.* But next time invariably brought the same scene.

She shook herself out of her paralysis and rushed the pick up the handset. "Hello?"

"Willow, let me speak to Sam." Darla Russell—the former Mrs. Samuel Russell, who had stepped in after Willow's mother died—didn't waste time with friendly greetings.

"Dad's not here right now," Willow hedged. Let the sheriff or one of his men give her stepmother the news that her ex-husband was dead. Willow had made a policy to say as little as possible to Darla and she saw no reason to deviate now.

"Well, where is he?" Darla demanded.

"I don't know." That much was the truth, at least.

"When you see him, tell him to call me. Right away."

"Okay."

"Don't forget, okay? This is important."

"Sure. Goodbye." Willow hung up the phone and stared at the white plastic handset, amber around the edges with age. She could call people her father knew and try to find out what he might have been up to. She should call a friend and ask for help.

But she had no friends in Eagle Mountain anymore. She knew most of the neighbors, of course.

She had grown up with them and with their sons and daughters, a few of whom had even stayed in the area. But she had not spoken to any of them in years and felt no connection.

When she did run into one of them in town, they were polite, even friendly, but she could feel all the questions behind the greetings—*What brought you home after so long? What happened to you in that eastern city?* A few of them were more direct.

We sure were surprised to hear you were back in town, Shayla Wayne had said at the grocery store last week. *I was sure once you left you'd never come back.*

Willow had believed that, too. There was nothing for her here in Eagle Mountain. She had only returned because she had no place left to go.

WILLOW RUSSELL'S FACE stayed with Chris as he left the Russell's Double R ranch and headed back toward town—a beautiful face full of pride and grief. Pain showed clearly in her eyes, but she fought against it, determined to stand strong.

After the ambulance had arrived and collected Sam Russell's body, the sheriff dismissed Chris. "You have things to do," he said. "Don't let me keep you from them."

Chris wanted to point out that, while his primary duties were related to the water district, he was still a fully certified deputy, able to do the law enforcement work of any other deputy. Travis must have read the sentiment on his face. "Depending on what Butch finds, I may need you on this investigation," he said. "Meanwhile, keep your ears open among the other ranchers you call on. Could be one of them knows something about this."

Right now, however, Chris wasn't on his way to a ranch, but to a new housing development in the shadow of Dakota Ridge. A rancher in the area had reported decreased water flows and the ditch rider had noted the same. After checking for leaks or blockages and finding none, the ditch rider had contacted Chris. "I think we probably have a home-owner in one of those new houses out there who needs a little education on Colorado water laws," the rider, Shirley Jacobson, had said. "It sounds better coming from you than from me."

Chris had been down this road before. Colorado water law was convoluted and complex. The rules regarding who had rights to water in the state dated back to the Gold Rush and seldom made sense to anyone who hadn't spent years studying the subject.

He followed the river for several miles, then turned in at a large granite sign proclaiming Welcome to Idlewilde Estates. He drove slowly past large lots with stucco or log homes set back from the road in groves of cottonwood or aspen trees that thrived along the banks of the Daimler Ditch. The ditch was one of a network of irrigation canals, some of them a hundred years old, that crisscrossed the county, carrying water from the Ute River and Centennial and Skyrocket creeks to area farmers and ranchers and a few residential water systems.

He spotted what he was looking for at the sixth house along the canal—a row of sunflowers along a back fence, fronted by a jungle of colorful blooms. He parked in the driveway of the house and walked around the side to get a better look. Drip irrigation hoses threaded through the plants and he could hear the chug of a pump.

A small white dog woke from a nap beneath a swing and began barking furiously. An attractive older woman, long gray curls pulled back from her face, emerged from the house and stared at him. "Who are you?" she demanded, fear tingeing the words.

"Deputy Chris Delray, Rayford County Sheriff's Department." He held out his identification. "I need to ask you a few questions, Miss…?"

"Howell. Melissa Howell." She walked out to the edge of the porch to meet him.

"I was noticing this irrigation setup you have," he said.

"Yes. What about it?"

"I'd like to take a closer look at it," he said, already moving toward the sound of the pump.

She followed him, the dog at her side. "Is there something wrong, Deputy?" she asked.

He walked to the edge of the ditch, and the hose leading from a submersible pump in the water. He reached down and hit the off switch, silencing the pump.

"Why did you do that?" she asked.

"You're not allowed to take any water from this

ditch, ma'am," Chris said. "The water rights belong to a rancher downstream from here."

"But the ditch is on my property," she said. "And there's plenty of water in there. It doesn't hurt anyone if I use a little."

To her, it was perfectly logical. But logic didn't always dictate Colorado water law. "The ditch belongs to the irrigation district," he said. "They have an easement through your property. You're not allowed to use the water and if you continue to do so, you could be fined up to seven hundred and fifty dollars a day, and you could even face time in jail."

She stared at him, mouth agape in disbelief.

"Do you understand, ma'am?" Chris asked. "You can't use this water. For anything."

"But if I don't water my flowers, they'll die," she said.

"I'm very sorry about that, ma'am. I can give you the name of a bulk water supplier. You can install a water tank and he'll deliver water to fill it. You can water your flowers from that tank." He took a business card from his wallet and handed it to her.

She frowned. "That sounds expensive."

"It's not too bad," he said. He looked down at the pump. "You need to disconnect all of this right away. I'll be checking back, and if I find this hooked up, I'll have to issue a citation."

"This is ridiculous," she said, anger replacing shock. "I never heard of such a thing."

"Where are you from?" he asked.

"Florida."

He nodded. "I understand in Florida they have more water than they know what to do with, but it's a different situation here, and the laws are different."

"I'm going to contact my lawyer about this," she said.

"Please do." Chris took out his ticket book and began writing. "Maybe he can help you understand the situation."

"What are you doing?" she asked.

"I'm issuing you a warning. It states you need to cease taking water from this ditch immediately or you'll be fined." He tore off the ticket and pressed it into her hand.

"I'll have to wait until my husband gets home to unhook everything," she said. "There's no way I can lift that heavy pump."

"I'll get it for you." That wasn't in his job description, but he doubted the woman's husband was much younger than her, and it was a heavy pump to haul uphill. He inched his way down to the edge of the ditch and crouched, prepared to heave the pump out, when a flash of something caught his eye. Gold metal, glittering bright in the clear water.

Ignoring the pump for the time being, he knelt beside the ditch and plunged his arm into the surprisingly cold water. The water reached past his elbow, soaking the short sleeve of his uniform shirt as his fingers closed around the item. He brought it up and dropped it on the bank beside him.

The little watch, bright gold and as big around as a plum, was worn smooth across the cover, the etched design so faded Chris couldn't tell what it was supposed to be. With the knuckle of one finger, he nudged it over, and stared at the initials embossed on the back side. *SRR* in elaborate script. Samuel Russell?

He did a quick calculation. This section of the ditch was maybe two miles from the place where Russell had been found. How had it not been caught in a gate between there and here? He pulled out his cell phone. The signal here was strong, and he dialed the sheriff's direct number.

"What you got, Chris?" Travis answered.

"I'm on a call in Idlewilde Estates." He gave the address. "I found something in the Daimler Ditch that runs in back of the property that you probably need to see."

He ended the call, and stared at the watch, gleaming in the sun. *How did you get all the way out here?* he wondered.

Chapter Three

Willow stared at the gold watch, shining in Deputy Delray's palm like a big gold button. "Yes, that's my father's watch." She looked up, into his serious brown eyes. "Where did you find it?"

He laid the watch, in a clear plastic evidence bag, on the kitchen counter between them. "First, where were you this morning between 5:00 a.m. and 7:30 a.m.?"

"I was here—asleep, most of that time."

"Is there anyone who can verify that?"

"What are you saying? Do you think *I* killed my father?" Tears stung her eyes, as much from anger as sorrow.

"Is there anyone who can confirm that you were home during that time?" he asked again.

"I sleep alone, Deputy," she snapped.

Something flickered behind those serious eyes—embarrassment? Amusement? She didn't care. "Where did you find that watch?" she asked again.

"The watch was found behind a house in Idlewilde Estates. In the irrigation canal."

She had a vague idea of the location of the fancy

new housing development on what had once been farmland. "How did it get there?" she asked.

"Did your father have the watch with him when he left the house this morning?" Delray asked.

"If he was awake and dressed, he had that watch." She looked away, fighting emotion again. "My mother gave it to him." Her father's first wife, the woman he had really loved, and would still be married to if she had lived. That was the story Willow always told herself, the only one she would believe.

"Can you think of any reason your father would have been near Idlewilde Estates this morning?" the deputy asked.

"No." She studied him, trying to decide if it would be worth trying to make him understand. He was watching her, too, as if waiting for her to say more. Fine. She'd give him a chance. "My father worked his whole life on this ranch," she said. "This *was* his life. And it's a lot of work, running a place like this. He had a routine. He got up early, had a cup of coffee, then went out to work. He would check on the cattle, or ride fence, or see to the irrigation ditches, or supervise a work crew—whatever needed doing. He would come back to the house about eight, eat breakfast, and go out to work some more. Some days he worked until dark. Other days, when it wasn't so busy, he would come in during the hottest part of the day and rest. Sometimes he went into town to run errands, but that was in the afternoon, after the work on the ranch was done. He didn't have a reason to go anywhere else that early in the day. And

I can't imagine he'd ever have a reason to go over to that development. Whose house was the watch found behind?"

"Melissa and Doug Howell. Did your father know them?"

"I don't think so. I never heard him mention them."

He looked away from her, at the living room that looked nothing like it had when she was a girl. Darla had redecorated after she moved in, and though she and Sam had divorced three years before, he hadn't bothered to replace anything. So the white leather sofas, plush red chairs and chrome-and-glass tables remained, amid piles of ranch catalogs, bits of old harness and the globe Willow had given her dad for Father's Day. "Did your father leave a note when he left this morning?" the deputy asked.

"No. He didn't feel the need to tell me where he was going or what he was doing." She had asked him to keep her informed, but he had scoffed at the idea, so she had let it drop.

The deputy's gaze met hers once more, softer this time. "Have you looked on his desk or in his bedroom for a note?"

His meaning hit her like a punch, and she took a step back. "Do you mean a suicide note?"

He nodded. "You should probably look. Or I can do it, if you'd rather."

"How long have you lived in Rayford County?" she asked him. She couldn't recall seeing him around when she lived here before, and she thought she would remember. Chris Delray was a good-looking man, clean-cut and fit, with a bit more polish than the boys she had grown up with. The kind of man women noticed.

"A couple of months," he said.

"Then you don't know my father. You don't know the kind of man he is—was." She swallowed. "He wouldn't take his own life. And he had no reason to. It doesn't make sense."

"So no financial problems? No health problems?"

"None. The ranch was doing well. And I nagged him into getting his first physical in five years recently and afterward he bragged about how the doctor said he was in better shape than men twenty years younger. He never took any medication stronger than an aspirin."

"What about relationship problems?" He looked around the room again. "You mentioned your mother. Is she no longer in the picture?"

"My mother died when I was thirteen. My dad remarried after I left for college, but they were only together six years. Since then he hasn't dated anyone that I'm aware of."

"Do you know of anyone who would want to kill him?"

"No!" She clenched her hands in frustration. "I'm not saying he was a saint, or that everyone loved him, but why would someone want to murder him?"

"Who inherits the ranch?" he asked.

"I assume I do. I'll have to speak to his lawyer."

The idea exhausted her. What did she want with the place, especially without her dad here?

"You don't know for sure?"

"Why should I? Do you know the terms of your parents' wills?"

He looked uncomfortable. "No."

"I'm his only child, and I never heard him talk about leaving the place to anyone else, but he was free to make his own decisions."

"What kind of work do you do?" he asked.

The shift in topic caught her off guard. Her cheeks grew hot. "I'm unemployed at the moment."

"What did your father think about you coming back here to live?" Delray asked.

"He was happy to have me here." Which was partly true. Dad didn't like her tendency to fuss over him.

If you're going to stay here, you need to find something to focus on besides me, he had said only the night before.

"I haven't moved back permanently," she said. "I'm only using this as a base while I look for a new job."

"What kind of work did you do?"

"I taught cultural anthropology at Hemphill University, in Connecticut." Her father, though proud of her education, had also believed she had chosen a particularly useless career. He would have preferred she study business, or veterinary medicine—something that would have been useful to him on the ranch.

"What will you do now that your father is gone?" the deputy asked. "Will you continue to operate the ranch?"

"I don't know. I haven't had time to think about that." The ranch was her father's most prized possession, not hers—but it was also a big part of her life. Her heritage. She couldn't imagine simply letting it slip away.

"It's a big place," he said. "I imagine you'll need help."

"My father has employees. They do most of the heavy lifting, though Dad would have hated to admit that."

Deputy Delray took out his phone. "What are their names? I may want to speak with them."

"Von King is the only full-time hand right now. There are a few other men who work during haying, or when it's time to move cattle, but they aren't employed right now."

"What does Von King do?"

"Whatever needs doing. He was cleaning and sharpening tools at the machine shed earlier."

Delray tucked his phone away. "Maybe I'll stop and talk with him on my way out."

"I haven't told him yet that Dad is…is dead." Saying the word was harder than she had expected.

"Why not?" Delray asked.

"I was upset and I didn't want to talk about it." She didn't want to talk about it now, with him, but she had no choice.

"I can tell him, if that would be easier for you."

The kindness in his voice caught her off guard. Up until now, he had seemed so businesslike, even accusatory. "I should do it," she said.

"You don't have to."

"I'll go with you and tell him, then you can talk to him." Having him there, adding authority to her words, might help. She feared that knowing her father was gone, Von would see her as vulnerable. She wasn't, but she didn't want the hassle of making that clear to him, not with everything else she had to deal with now.

They walked together to the machine shed. She was very aware of him beside her, the way he shortened his stride to match her own, the solid bulk of him casting a shadow over her, his calmness.

Von was sharpening the point of a pickax on a grinder and didn't notice when they first entered the shed. Delray stepped to one side, casting a shadow across the workbench, and Von looked up and took them in. He returned to his work and a full minute passed before he shut off the grinder and turned to them. "What is it?" he asked.

"This is Deputy Delray," Willow said. "I'm afraid my father..." What? Had an accident? Was killed? She tried to force the words past the knot in her throat and couldn't.

"Samuel Russell died earlier this morning," Deputy Delray said. "His body was found in one of the irrigation ditches."

Von's face registered no emotion. "That's too bad," he said.

"Did you see Mr. Russell this morning?" Delray asked.

Von shook his head. "Nope. The only person I saw was her." He pointed the pickax at Willow. "Leaving early in Sam's truck."

She froze. Was Von accusing her of something? She couldn't look at the deputy, afraid of what she might see in his expression.

"When was the last time you saw Mr. Russell?" Delray asked.

"Yesterday, before supper," Von said. "He told me he wanted all the hand tools cleaned and sharpened today." He studied the point of the pickax.

"What was his mood?" Delray asked.

Von shrugged. "He seemed normal to me."

"He wasn't upset about anything?"

"He was a pretty grumpy old coot most of the time, anyway," Von said. His gaze flickered to her and she wondered if he had intended to hurt her with the criticism of her father.

"Where were you between five and seven thirty this morning?" Delray asked.

"I got up at six, had breakfast and came here to work," Von said.

"Where do you live?"

Von turned to Willow. "She can tell you that."

She wanted to refuse to take part in whatever game Von was playing, but the deputy was looking at her, expectant. "He lives in a cabin a couple of miles from here," she said. "You passed the entrance on the way in."

"Is there anyone who can verify your alibi?" Delray asked.

Von snorted. "Am I being accused of some crime?"

"Is there anyone who will confirm your whereabouts this morning?" Delray asked again.

"No."

Delray turned to leave and Willow hurried after him. They had only taken a few steps when Von called after them. "How did he die?"

"We're still waiting on the coroner's ruling," Delray said.

Von grunted. Before they were out the door, Willow heard the grinder start up again.

"What's his story?" Delray asked. "How long has he worked here?"

"He's been here about nine months, I think," she said. "The man who worked for Dad before moved back to New Mexico to work on his family's ranch. I'm not sure how Dad found Von."

"What's his background? Do you know?"

"Dad told me he'd been in prison."

Delray's gaze sharpened. "Your dad didn't have a problem with that?"

"He said everybody deserved a second chance. And he said Von is a good worker."

"Are you comfortable, having him around?"

Again, his kindness touched a soft place inside her she didn't want to reveal. "I'll be all right. I know how to take care of myself."

He took a business card from his shirt pocket and

passed it to her. "If there's any trouble, call me," he said.

She nodded, and then stood on the front steps and watched while he got into his SUV and left. She didn't know what to make of the deputy, who had all but accused her of having a good reason to want her father dead one minute, and had handled the exchange with Von with sensitivity. He'd said to call him if she had trouble, but she could have told him she had had nothing but trouble over the past few months. She had hoped coming home would give her space to regroup and refocus, to get her life back on the right track. That wasn't happening. Without her father here, she was more lost than ever.

"HE WAS SHOT with his own gun, at close range." Dr. Butch Collins indicated the wound on Samuel Russell's body with the tip of a felt-tip pen. The sheriff had invited Chris to accompany him to the medical examiner's office in the basement of the hospital the next morning. It was Wednesday, and Chris was trying to focus on the injury as separate from the man whose daughter he had spoken to only hours before. He'd seen death before, but never this naked and clinical. It wasn't a usual part of his job.

"How do you know it was his gun?" Chris asked.

"His name's engraved on it," Butch said. "And I've been pheasant hunting with Sam Russell. I know that weapon."

"So, is it suicide?" Chris asked.

Butch looked to the sheriff, who stood across from

Chris and the doctor, on the other side of the body. "What do you think, Travis?"

"I'm waiting for you to tell me," Sheriff Travis Walker said.

"Then take a look at this." Butch walked to the top of the exam table, and tilted Russell's head to one side. "You see that bruising?" he asked. "There, under the hair."

Chris forced himself to look, at the pattern of darkened flesh beneath Russell's thick white hair. "What's that from?" he asked.

"Somebody hit him with something heavy and flat—a board, a big flat rock—not sure."

"Hard enough to knock him down?" Travis asked.

"Hard enough to knock him out," Butch said. "The bruising isn't just external. There's a cerebral hemorrhage under there."

"Could it have happened after he was shot?" Chris asked. "He fell back and hit his head on a rock or something?"

Butch shook his head. "He was found facedown in that ditch, right? And I checked the scene and didn't see any rocks that could have done this damage. One more thing." He moved to Russell's hands. At the scene, the techs had slipped a plastic bag over each hand to preserve any evidence. The hands were bare now. "No residue on his hands from firing a weapon recently," Butch said. "But dirt and scratches, the kind I'd expect if he fell back and tried to catch himself, maybe thrashed around a little before he lost consciousness."

"So—somebody hit him over the head, then while he was out, took his gun and shot him?" Chris asked.

"Then arranged his body in the ditch with the gun beneath him to make it look like suicide," Butch said.

"Anything else you can tell us?" Travis asked.

"Whoever shot Sam Russell was standing very close," Butch said. "If he didn't get blood on him at the time of the shooting, it would have been hard to avoid it when he—or she—moved the body and arranged it in the ditch."

"I guess his daughter was right when she insisted her father wouldn't kill himself," Chris said.

"A lot of people say that," the sheriff said. "Most of the time it isn't true." He looked at Russell's body. "Maybe this time it is."

"Sam Russell didn't take his own life," Butch said. "You two have a murder on your hands."

Those words still rang in Chris's ears as he walked out of the hospital with Travis. "Do you want to be part of this investigation?" the sheriff asked when they reached the parking lot. "Technically, you were hired to primarily deal with water issues, and back up other cases. But your experience dealing with local ranchers could be helpful."

"I can handle my water work and this investigation, too," Chris said. His job kept him busy, but it wasn't overly demanding. "I feel like I'm already in hip-deep, anyway."

The sheriff nodded. "You talked to Willow Russell more than any of us. What's your feel for her? Does she have a motive to kill her father?"

"She's unemployed, recently moved back home. She says she doesn't know the terms of her father's will, but she's his only child, so it stands to reason she would inherit at least part of the ranch. She says she was home alone this morning, but no one can verify that." He rubbed the back of his neck. "On the other hand, she insisted her father's death wasn't suicide, and urged us to find his murderer."

"He turned his back on whoever hit him, so he probably knew and trusted them, or at least didn't suspect any ill will," Travis said. "But she's not a big woman, and it takes some force to knock a man out. Sam was older, but I wouldn't call him frail."

"She wouldn't be my primary suspect," Chris said.

"Who would that be?"

"He's got a hired hand, an ex-con named Von King. Struck me as a generally unpleasant fellow. He doesn't have anyone to vouch for his alibi, either. I'm not sure what he would stand to gain from killing his boss, however. He did say Russell was a 'grumpy old coot.'"

"Check into him. You should also question Trey Allerton. He's leasing a section of the Russell ranch and living in a trailer on the property with a woman named Courtney Baker and her little girl."

"I remember," Chris said. "He was linked to Talia Larrivee's murderer somehow, right?" Chris hadn't been actively involved in that investigation the month previous, but he had heard plenty of talk.

"Talia's killer, Tom Chico, and Allerton were

business partners in the lease with Russell, and supposedly Allerton plans to build a summer camp–type ranch for disadvantaged youth," Travis said. "But I haven't seen much sign of progress."

"Why would he want to kill Russell?" Chris asked.

"That's what I want you to find out," Travis said. "Take Shane with you. He worked the Larrivee murder and knows Allerton and can fill you in."

Chris rode with Travis back to the sheriff's department, making a mental list of everything he needed to do. He planned to start with pulling Von King's criminal record, but before he could make it to his desk, office manager Adelaide Kinkaid waylaid him and the sheriff. "There's someone here to see you, Sheriff." Adelaide, a white-haired dynamo who wore outlandish earrings and bright colors, kept the office running smoothly. She knew everyone and everything in town and as the widow of a police officer, had a firm grasp on the way law enforcement was supposed to work.

Chris turned away, but Adelaide reached out and snagged him. "She wants to talk to you, too. About Sam Russell."

Chris followed Travis toward the front lobby of the building. A well-preserved older woman with a cap of black hair and deep lines on either side of her mouth stood at their approach. "I'm Darla Russell," she said. "And I want to know what happened to my husband."

Chapter Four

"I don't think much of local law enforcement. They wouldn't tell me anything about Sam's death, despite the fact that I'm his widow." Darla Russell made this announcement approximately two minutes after dropping her suitcases in the middle of the ranch house living room Wednesday afternoon. She and her adult son, Emmet, had arrived less than a day after guilt had induced Willow to call and inform her former stepmother of Sam's passing.

"But you're his ex-wife, not his widow," Willow said. She still stood by the door, wishing she had never opened it to these two.

Darla drew herself up to her full five foot nine, the teased bouffant of her ink-black hair adding a couple of inches. "Neither Sam nor I ever remarried," she said. "I think that entitles me to call myself his widow."

This wasn't worth arguing over. "What are you two doing here?" Willow asked. She glanced at Emmet, who had already settled on the sofa, his long legs stretched out in front of him. Twenty-nine years old, pale and sullen, what hair he had left in a bad comb-over, Emmet was perpetually "between jobs" and lived with his mother in Albuquerque.

"Someone has to get to the bottom of this," Darla said. "The police never tell the family anything in cases like this unless someone holds their feet to the fire. Besides, Sam would have wanted me here with you."

"Thank you, but I'm fine on my own."

"Don't be ridiculous." Darla sat in the recliner—Sam's chair. Willow wanted to tell her to move, but didn't have the energy for the argument that was sure to ensue. "The first thing you need to do is contact that pretty-boy sheriff and tell him he has your permission to share details of the case with me. They have you listed as Sam's next of kin."

Because I am his next of kin, she thought, but didn't waste her breath pointing this out. "I really don't think you need to bother with all this," she said instead. "You should go home and I promise to let you know if anything happens that affects you."

"You don't think Sam's death affects me?" Her voice rose and inwardly, Willow cringed. "Sam was the love of my life and I will mourn him forever. I don't know how you can be so cold. I did my best to be a good mother to you and this is how you repay me." She dug a tissue from her purse and pressed it to her eyes.

Willow had been twenty and away at college when Sam married Darla. She hadn't needed a mother and had only interacted with Darla and her son on holidays and brief visits home. What she had seen then hadn't impressed her, though she had told herself that if this woman made her father happy, it was none of Willow's concern. When Sam and Darla had divorced, Willow had been relieved, if a little sad for her father. She didn't need, or want, Darla and Emmet here now. "It was very kind of you to travel all this way to help me," Willow said. "But there really isn't anything you can do. Until the sheriff's department has finished their investigation, we can't even plan a funeral service."

"We were already in the area," Darla said. "When I called yesterday morning, it was to tell Sam we were coming for a visit." She narrowed her eyes. "Did you know then that Sam was dead? And you didn't tell me?"

"I had just found out," Willow said. "I was still in shock."

Darla seemed to consider this, then patted the sofa cushion beside her. "Sit down and tell me what happened."

Reluctantly, Willow sat on the end of the sofa. "I told you on the phone last night that the ditch rider found Dad in the irrigation ditch near the loading chute and cattle pens," she said.

"You said he'd been shot. But who shot him?"

"I don't know." Willow shook her head. "That's what the sheriff is trying to find out."

"And how long is that going to take?" Darla asked.

"I don't know," Willow said again. "I can't think of anyone who would want to kill Dad." She didn't mention suicide. No matter what Deputy Delray said, she couldn't believe her father would take his own life.

"Can they issue a death certificate without knowing who killed him?" Darla asked.

Willow frowned. "I have no idea. Why do you ask?"

"You have to have a death certificate in order for the will to go to probate," Emmet said. Willow stared at him. He shrugged. "I'm just saying."

"Have you looked at the will yet?" Darla asked.

"No. Dad has only been gone a day."

"There's nothing to be gained in putting it off," Darla said. "And I suppose you've already looked for any cash he kept around." She turned her head to survey the living room.

"What cash?" Willow asked.

Darla fixed her gaze on Willow once more. "Sam always kept cash on hand. In case of emergency."

"I'm sure he had some money in his wallet," Willow said. "But I guess the sheriff still has that." She'd have to ask next time she spoke to someone from the sheriff's office.

"I'm not talking about a few bills in his wallet," Darla said. "I'm talking hundreds, probably thousands of dollars Sam kept here."

"Do you mean in the safe?" Willow didn't remember her father keeping cash in there, but maybe he had started to do so. She hadn't thought to look.

"Not in the safe," Darla said. "He kept the money hidden."

“Where did he hide it?” Willow said. “This is the first I’ve heard of it.”

“You didn’t know?” Darla widened her eyes. “I thought everyone knew. Sam had quite the reputation as a bit of a miser.”

This was the first Willow had heard of this. Yes, Sam was frugal, but she had never thought of him as stingy. “So you saw him hide money?” she asked.

Darla pressed her lips together, the lines on either side of her mouth deepening. “Well, no, I didn’t actually see him. But other people told me about it.”

“What other people?” Willow couldn’t believe this.

“Oh, just people.” Darla waved her hand. “My hairdresser mentioned it, and one of the ranch hands said something about it. I asked Sam about it, but of course he denied it. But he would, wouldn’t he? I mean, the whole point of hiding the money was to keep other people from finding it.”

“I don’t think Dad hid money around here,” Willow said. “I’ve never found any of it. Besides, what difference does it make to you?” She was weary of making nice to this annoying woman.

“Don’t get ugly with me,” Darla said. “For your information, Sam promised Emmet a share of this ranch when Sam passed on. And I think that includes any cash you find.”

The idea was so outrageous Willow couldn’t breathe for a few seconds. “Why would my father leave part of the ranch to Emmet?” she asked.

“We negotiated it as part of the divorce,” Darla

said. "I wouldn't ask for spousal support if he agreed to leave half of the Double R to Emmet."

She couldn't believe her father would do such a thing, but then, she still couldn't understand what Sam had seen in Darla in the first place. "Why would Emmet even want half the ranch?" she asked.

"All this real estate must be worth a lot of money," Emmet said. "I figure I could sell it."

She swallowed down a wave of nausea. Her father would be horrified at the idea. "I'll have to speak to Dad's lawyer," Willow said.

"I can call him." Darla pulled out her phone. "What's his name and number?"

Willow was about to refuse when her own phone buzzed. She slid it from her pocket and didn't recognize the local number. "Hello?" She stood and walked out of the room, the phone pressed tightly to her ear.

"Hello, Willow? It's Chris Delray."

She entered the kitchen and shut the door behind her. "Deputy Delray. What can I do for you?"

"The coroner has made his report and I wanted you to know before we release anything to the press."

Fear climbed her throat. "What did he say?"

"I'm sorry to tell you that your father was murdered."

Hearing the word out loud, instead of only in her head, shocked her more than she would have thought possible. She groped for a kitchen chair and sank into it, and clamped one hand over her mouth, trying to hold back a sob. "I'm sorry," Delray continued. "Losing a loved one is hard enough. Losing them to murder is that much worse. We'll be doing everything we can to find his killer. I'll probably have more questions for you soon."

"Thank you," she managed to choke out the words.

"Are you going to be all right? Is there anyone I can call to come be with you?"

"I'm okay." She struggled to pull herself together. "Dad's ex-wife is here. She and her son just showed up a few minutes ago."

"They stopped by the sheriff's office," he said. "She wasn't too happy when the sheriff told her he couldn't release any information to her."

"So she said."

"Well, it's good that you're not alone right now."

"I'd rather be alone. I think she only came here because she has a crazy idea that my dad left half the ranch to her son."

"I'm sorry you're having to deal with that on top of grieving for your father and answering all our questions," he said. "If you like, I could come over and question her and her son. I could annoy them into leaving."

She almost smiled at the image of him doing just that. "Thanks, but I can deal with them. It's a good distraction."

"I'll be in touch," he said. "Call me if you need anything."

It was something people said to the bereaved, but she thought Deputy Delray might mean it.

She tucked her phone back in her pocket and went

to the sink and filled a glass with water. While she drank it, she watched out the window as Darla, trailed by Emmet, crossed the yard toward Von King, who had just emerged from the equipment shed. Willow couldn't hear the conversation, but body language told the story. Darla gestured with both arms held wide. Von scowled and shook his head. Darla, hands on hips, unleashed another torrent of words. Von waved his arms and stormed off.

A few minutes later Darla, minus Emmet, burst into the kitchen. "You need to fire that insolent hired hand. He called me a very ugly word just now."

"What did you say to upset him?" Willow asked.

"I told him I wanted him to give us a tour of the property, and he refused."

"He has work to do," Willow said. "He's not a tour guide."

"He doesn't have to be rude," Darla said.

"I guess Dad didn't hire him for his personality."

Darla folded her arms over her chest. "Then you can show us around the ranch. I want to see what Sam did with the place since I lived here."

Willow set the empty water glass in the sink and turned to face Darla. "I have other things I need to do now," she said. She needed to call her father's lawyer, and she needed to take something for the headache hammering in her skull. She moved past Darla, toward the door.

"I don't understand why you have to be so unfriendly," Darla said. "I blame your father for not remarrying sooner after your mother died. A woman would have taught you that charm is the most powerful weapon a woman can have. It's no wonder you've failed to attract a man."

"I guess lack of charm explains why Emmet is still single, too," Willow said. She left before Darla could fire back a retort. She shouldn't let the woman get to her this way. She had a fight on her hands to keep the ranch and to help find out who had murdered her father. She couldn't let a couple of unpleasant not-quite-relatives distract her.

DEPUTY SHANE ELLIS was a former major-league pitcher who had been sidelined by a career-ending injury, returned to his hometown of Eagle Mountain and signed on with the sheriff's department. That was all Chris knew about his fellow officer, except that Shane had been involved in the hunt for Talia Larrivee's killer the month before, while Chris had been primarily focused on working with local ranches during the busy summer irrigation season.

"How much did the sheriff tell you about Trey Allerton?" Shane asked as he rode with Chris toward the Russell ranch Wednesday afternoon.

"He said Allerton was leasing part of the ranch from Russell, and that he planned to build some kind of summer camp for kids?"

"I learned more about him when my fiancée, Lauren, asked me to help her find her former sister-in-law, Courtney Baker, and Courtney's daughter, Ashlyn. Supposedly Allerton and Courtney want to build a camp where kids who've experienced some kind of trauma can come and have a break," Shane said. "Horseback riding, hiking, counselors, that kind of thing. Sam Russell agreed to lease them part of the north section of the Double R."

"Did Allerton and Sam have a disagreement over the lease or something?" Chris asked.

"Not that I know of," Shane said. "But we'll want to ask about that."

"What's Allerton's connection to Talia's murder?" Chris asked. He should have paid more attention to that case, but it wasn't his, so he hadn't memorized the details.

"Allerton was supposedly business partners with Tom Chico, the man who admitted to killing Talia," Shane said. "Chico and Talia hung out with Allerton and Courtney for a couple of weeks before Talia disappeared. Tom Chico is a suspect in the murder of another young woman in Colorado Springs at the same time Allerton was stationed there. We think the two men might have met up when they were both in Colorado Springs, but we haven't found any real proof of that."

"So Allerton may or may not have a questionable past," Chris said.

"Right. He doesn't have a criminal record that we're aware of, but he comes across as a schemer. He has big plans for this ranch, but so far he's mainly talking other people into giving him money."

"Some people call that good business," Chris said.

"Yeah, they do. And Sam seemed okay with Allerton, as long as he was paid what he was owed, which he was. But he's worth questioning, if only because he and Courtney live closest to Russell's ranch house."

They passed the entrance to the Russell ranch. Chris couldn't see much from the road—the ranch house itself was much farther up the drive. He wondered how Willow was faring with her stepmother, who had come across in the sheriff's department as loud and demanding—the opposite of Willow.

But soft-spoken wasn't the same as weak. So far, Willow had radiated strength and determination. In a war of wills, Chris would bet on Sam's daughter as the winner.

A few miles farther on, Shane turned the cruiser into a second drive, this one pocked with deep ruts. He stopped the cruiser in front of an old mobile home with turquoise siding, a small wooden landing and steps sitting crookedly in front of the door. "It doesn't look as if they've done anything in the three weeks since I was up here," Shane said. He and Chris got out and made their way to the door.

The door rattled in its frame when Shane knocked, and a few moments later, heavy footsteps inside moved toward them. The door opened and a tall, broad-shouldered man with sandy brown hair looked out at them. "Hello," he said, his voice without inflection.

"Hello, Trey," Shane said. "This is Deputy Delray. We wanted to ask you and Courtney a few questions."

"Courtney isn't here," he said. "What is this about?"

"Can we come in?" Shane asked. "This won't take long."

Allerton hesitated, then held the door open wider. "Sure."

The interior of the trailer was clean, but worn. The sofa sagged and the only other seating was a single folding chair. Allerton picked up a blanket from the floor in front of the sofa. "I was taking a nap," he said, and sank onto the sofa.

Shane perched on the other end of the sofa and Chris took the folding chair. "Did you know Sam Russell died yesterday morning?" Shane asked.

"Von King was by here late yesterday and he told us." Allerton sat forward, clasped hands on one knee. "He said the old guy killed himself."

"He didn't kill himself," Chris said. "He was murdered."

Allerton sat up straighter. "Really? Who did it?"

"We're trying to find out," Chris said. "Have you heard of any disagreements between Sam Russell and anyone else?"

Allerton shook his head. "I didn't know him all that well."

"But you're leasing this land from him," Chris said.

"Yeah, but that's just business. It's not like we were friends or anything."

"Are you friends with Von King?" Shane asked.

"He's done some work for us around the place, that's all."

"How do you know Von?" Chris asked.

"I told Mr. Russell I was looking for someone to help with some cleanup and stuff around here and he told me I could hire Von, so I did."

"Where were you between five and seven thirty yesterday morning?" Chris asked.

Allerton didn't appear surprised or upset by the question. "I was here. In bed."

"Is there anyone who can verify that?" Chris asked.

"Courtney will. She was with me."

"Where is Courtney?" Shane asked.

"She and her little girl took some laundry to town, and planned to buy some groceries."

"Lauren would like to see her and Ashlyn," Shane said.

"That's up to Courtney," Allerton said. He stood. "Sorry I can't help you with the whole Russell mystery. I'm too busy here to pay attention to what's going on with other people."

Chris and Shane stood also, and followed Allerton to the door. "How is the youth ranch coming?" Shane asked. "Have you started building yet?"

"It's a slow process," Allerton said. "But I'm courting an investor and that should give us the money we need soon. It's going to be great."

Neither officer said anything until they were back on the road. "Courtney was married to Lauren's brother, Mike," Shane said. "He was killed in Afghanistan and the two women were close until Courtney took up with Allerton and she and her daughter, Ashlyn, moved here. Allerton says he was Lauren's brother's best friend, but Lauren never heard him mention Trey."

"I'll ask Sam's daughter what she knows about her father's relationship with Allerton," Chris said. Trey Allerton hadn't impressed him as the kind of person who could pull off a big project like his proposed youth ranch, but that didn't make him a murderer.

"I think it's suspicious that Allerton is pals with Tom Chico, a murderer who has a pretty long rap sheet," Shane said. "And now he's pals with Von King, another ex-con."

"Sam Russell told Willow that Von had been in prison," Chris said. "But when I tried to find information about him, I drew a blank."

"It's not the sort of thing a person lies about to impress a potential employer," Shane said.

"Maybe King heard Sam had a soft spot for excons," Chris said. "He had supposedly hired them before."

"Or maybe Von King isn't his real name," Shane said.

"Sounds like we need to talk to him again," Chris said. "I want to interview the ex-wife and her son, too. Willow said they showed up today asking about the will. They said Sam promised to leave half the ranch to the son."

"People have killed for less," Shane said. "Let's stop by the ranch now and see what they have to say."

Chapter Five

"I was very sorry to hear of your father's death. Sam was a great man, and he will be missed by many in this community." Ted Delray, Attorney at Law, sounded suitably grave when he took Willow's call Wednesday afternoon.

She had been prepared to break the news to Ted herself, but apparently the community grapevine had already gotten the word out. "How did you find out about it?" she asked.

"It's on the newspaper's website," Ted said. "Murder is big news in a county this small. And even more shocking following the murder of that young woman last month. And your father was so well-known and well respected."

"Yes, it is shocking," she said.

"Does the sheriff have any idea who did it?" She heard the eagerness behind the question, and realized this was the first of many such inquiries from the people she knew. Murder held a fascination, and carried with it a desire to be a little closer to the mystery. Or maybe Ted had another reason for asking.

"Are you related to Chris Delray?" she asked. "He's a sheriff's deputy."

"Chris is my son," Ted said. "Is he involved in the murder investigation?"

"Yes." She wondered why Ted didn't know that. Then again, maybe Chris didn't talk about his work with his father.

"Was Chris able to tell you anything about who might have killed your father?" Ted asked.

"No one seems to know anything," she said. "I can't think of anyone who would want to harm Dad, much less kill him. Can you?"

"I can't. But a man doesn't get to be almost seventy without making a few enemies."

"Who were Dad's enemies?"

"Maybe *enemy* is too strong a word. But you know your father wasn't happy when the Carstairses sold the family ranch to that developer who built Idlewilde Estates. He and Bud Carstairs were good friends for years, but they never spoke to each other again after that."

"I heard Bud sold the place to pay for Mary Ann's care in that special Alzheimer's facility in Junction," Willow said.

"He did. But your father took a hard line about things like that."

"Bud Carstairs didn't murder my father." She pictured the neighboring rancher as he was the last time she had seen him—an almost elfin figure with a cap of white hair and a warm grin. When she was little, he would slip her sticks of the cinnamon chewing gum he carried with him since he'd given up tobacco years before.

"I'm sure he didn't," Ted said. "I'm just offering that as one example of how Sam had had disagreements with people that left hard feelings. Maybe there's something like that we don't know about."

"Maybe." Willow knew her father wasn't a saint, but had he really done something that made someone so angry that person decided to kill him? "That's not really why I called," she said. "I need to know about Dad's will."

"Of course. Well, I'll need a copy of the death certificate, and we'll go before a judge and ask her to issue letters testamentary, declaring you the executrix, which will give you authority to act on behalf of the estate. The will has to go through probate, but I can handle all of that for you."

It sounded overwhelming, but people dealt with this sort of thing every day, so she would, too. "Can you tell me the terms of the will?" she asked.

Ted paused, so long she wondered if they had lost the connection. "You don't know?" he finally asked.

"No." Her stomach roiled. This didn't sound good.

"I did advise Sam to discuss this with you, but as we've already talked about, he had very strong feelings about how things should be done, and no one could persuade him differently."

"What provisions did he make?" she asked, steeling herself for the worst.

"Several years ago—about the time they broke

ground for Idlewilde—your father placed the entire ranch in a conservation easement."

"What does that mean?"

"It means you are free to live on the ranch, to continue to operate it and derive income from it, but it cannot be divided or sold for any other purpose but ranching."

"Does any part of the ranch go to Emmet Caspar?"

"Who is Emmet Caspar?"

"Darla Caspar Russell's son from her first marriage," Willow said. "Darla was Dad's second wife."

"I know who Darla is," Ted said. "And she and her son aren't mentioned in the will. There is a small bequest to the county ranching museum and that's it. Everything else goes to you."

Willow sagged in her chair, weak with relief. "Darla is here now," she said. "She told me my father promised to leave half of the ranch to Emmet if she didn't ask for spousal support."

"I handled the divorce for your father and there was no such agreement. He did pay a generous settlement to her at the time of the divorce, as outlined in their prenup."

"Dad and Darla had a prenup?" She didn't know why the idea surprised her so much, except that her father—who had never owned a computer, or even a smartphone—had seemed so firmly fixed in the past, where things like prenuptial agreements didn't exist.

"Your father was a shrewd businessman," Ted said.

"I'm relieved to hear it," she said. "And I'm pleased about the conservation easement."

"Not everyone is," Ted said. "I've dealt with heirs who are absolutely furious they won't be able to make their fortunes by selling the family estate. So do you intend to stay and continue to operate the ranch yourself?"

"I don't know about that," she said.

"If you decide the day-to-day operation of the place isn't for you, I can put you in touch with some people who can help you find a manager," Ted said. "Or you can sell the property to someone who will continue to operate it as a ranch. They would still be bound by the terms of the conservation easement, but there are people who look for that kind of thing."

"I'll have to think about it awhile." She had never been that interested in ranching, but could she really sell off her father's legacy, even to another rancher?

"No rush. In fact, I would advise you not to make any hasty decisions. In the meantime, let me know when you have the official death certificate and I'll start the proceedings for probate."

"Thank you, Ted." She hung up the phone, feeling much less burdened. And she couldn't wait to find Darla and give her the good news.

CHRIS AND SHANE located Von King at the corrals and loading chute near where Sam's body had been found. Crime scene tape still fluttered from stakes around the irrigation ditch. Shane parked the sheriff's department SUV on the side of the road, behind

Von's truck, and they ducked under the barbed wire fencing to reach the ranch hand. "When I was driving by last night, I saw someone had cut this fence wire," Von said as they neared. He hammered a staple into a wooden fence post. "One of your crime scene people, I expect."

"Was the wire cut yesterday?" Shane asked Chris.

Chris shook his head. "I think Von's right, and the crime scene team cut it to get their equipment in. You can file a claim to get the sheriff's department to reimburse the ranch for the damage," he told Von.

"It's just wire and a few staples." Von tugged at the strand of wire, shiny against the rusted strands on either side of it. "What do you two want?"

"We've been talking to Trey Allerton," Shane said. "He told us you've been doing some work for him."

"I have." Von straightened and faced them. "What of it?"

"What kind of work?" Chris asked.

"Grunt work. Moving rocks and dirt, propping up broken-down fences."

"Did you know Tom Chico?" Shane asked.

"Never met him."

"He and Allerton were business partners," Shane said.

"Trey is the only one I dealt with. Don't know about the other guy." He moved along the fence, tugging at the wire at each post. Most people found being questioned by two uniformed officers unsettling, but not Von, maybe because he'd been questioned before.

"We know your real name isn't Von King," Chris said.

Von fixed him with a hard gaze. "My name is Von King. I can show you my driver's license if you like."

"There's no law against changing your name," Shane said. "We're just curious what you went by before."

"My name is Von King," he said again, and moved to the next section of fencing.

Chris and Shane exchanged a look, silently acknowledging this line of questioning was going nowhere. "How are things at the ranch house today?" Chris asked.

"The ex-wife and her boy showed up, circling like vultures."

"Did you know them when she was married to Sam before?" Shane asked.

"Wasn't around then. But she made a point of telling me they'd been married."

"When did she arrive at the ranch?" Shane asked.

"Around noon. The two of them moved in, suitcases and all, and she started giving orders."

"Had she visited the ranch before this?" Chris asked. "I mean, since you've worked for Sam?"

"Nope." He moved down the fence line and they followed.

"Did Sam ever mention anyone he had a disagreement with?" Chris asked. "Anyone he was angry at or worried about?"

"He wasn't my best friend, he was my boss," Von said. "We talked about the work he wanted me to do and when he wanted me to do it. We didn't stand around baring our souls."

"So you don't know anyone he argued with?" Chris pushed.

Von stopped, one hand on top of a fence post, and faced him. "He and Willow argued plenty," he said.

"What about?" Chris asked.

"I don't know. But I could hear the raised voices from the house. They were both yelling."

"When was this?" Shane asked.

"Night before last," Von said. "Right at dark. I went to put away the tools I'd been using, replacing some broken fence posts on the south pasture, and I heard them going at it."

"Did that alarm you?" Chris asked. "Hearing them fighting?"

"It wasn't the first time. And it wasn't any of my business, either." He turned away. "I've got work to do and I think you do, too." He didn't wait for an answer, simply walked away, long strides over the sagebrush-dotted ground until he reached his truck and climbed in.

"We'd better talk to Willow and find out what this argument was about," Shane said, leading the way to the cruiser.

"If Von was even telling the truth," Chris said.

"We have to check it out," Shane said. "If the two of them were arguing and the next morning Sam was killed, we can't ignore it."

"Of course not." So far, this was the first they had heard about Sam Russell arguing with anyone. It didn't mean Willow had murdered her father, but it did indicate she hadn't been entirely truthful with them, and that troubled him even more than doubts about her guilt or innocence.

WHEN WILLOW EMERGED from her bedroom after her telephone conversation with Ted Delray, she found Darla and Emmet in the living room, preparing to leave. "We're going into town to eat, since you haven't offered us anything," Darla said.

"Suit yourself."

"You don't have to be so rude!" Darla huffed.

The little patience Willow had left deserted her. "You're the one who's rude—showing up here uninvited," she said.

"We have every right to be here," Darla said.

"I don't think you do," Willow said. "I just got off the phone with Dad's lawyer."

"Oh?" Darla crossed her arms over her chest and looked at Willow expectantly. "What did he have to say?"

"We discussed the terms of Dad's will."

"And? Don't be coy, Willow. You're too old for it to be cute."

"Everything comes to me, and it's in a conservation easement so it can't be sold for development or divided."

She had expected Darla to be upset, maybe even

to fly into a rage. Instead, she uncrossed her arms and smiled. "There's another will," she said.

"There isn't," Willow said.

"There is." Emmet, who had been lurking behind his mother until this point, finally spoke. "Mom has a copy."

"I can show it to you, if you like," Darla said. "After we've returned from dinner."

"After you return from dinner, you can pack your bags and leave," Willow said. "My lawyer will be contacting you."

"You can't throw us out." Darla's veneer of calm cracked.

"I can and I am," Willow said. "This is my home, not yours."

"Your father would be appalled to know you were treating us this way," Darla said.

"Your ex-husband would never have let you in the door in the first place," Willow said.

"I can't believe this." Darla stood and faced Willow, who became very aware that this woman was six inches taller and probably fifty pounds heavier than her. "I came here to help you!" Darla's voice rose. "And this is how you repay me!"

Emmet stood, too. "You're upsetting Mother," he said.

Willow glared at the two of them. She wanted to tell them exactly what she thought of them, but that would only anger them more and escalate the situation. Instead, she took a deep breath and took out her phone. "There's a motel in Eagle Mountain," she said. "You can stay there, or you can go back to Albuquerque. But you have to leave. And if you don't, I'll call the sheriff."

She expected Darla to object again. "We'll talk in the morning," she said, and headed out of the room. "Emmet, come," she barked as she passed her son.

Willow stared at the closed door and listened to Darla's car starting up outside. She was probably stuck with those two for tonight, but in the morning she would make them leave, if she had to contact the sheriff's department for help. What would they think of this new family drama? she wondered.

She went into the kitchen and put water on to boil for tea. She should probably eat something, but she couldn't imagine what. She felt hollow inside, as if the loss of her father had left a vacancy she feared might never be filled. All she really wanted was to crawl into bed, pull the covers over her head and wake up tomorrow to find this was all a horrible nightmare.

She was staring into the refrigerator, seeing nothing, when she was startled by a knock on the back door.

"We saw you through the window, so I came around here," Deputy Delray said after she opened the door. Another officer stood at his shoulder, a good-looking man with blue eyes.

"Come in." She held the door open wider. "You may be just in time to help me."

The two moved past her, filling the small kitchen

with their bulk. "This is Deputy Ellis," Deputy Delray said.

The other officer nodded. "What do you need our help with?" Deputy Delray asked.

"I've just told my dad's ex-wife and her son that they need to leave," she said. "They said we'd talk more after they returned from eating in Eagle Mountain, which I suspect means I'm stuck with them one more night, but I'm going to try again in the morning. Can I call the sheriff's office if they give me trouble? I mean, if I don't want them here, they're trespassing, right?"

"What have they been doing that has you so upset?" Deputy Delray asked.

"I don't want them here. Isn't that enough?"

He nodded, those warm brown eyes studying her. She felt that gaze, as if he was trying to see past the surface to what lay beneath. "Have they done something in particular to upset you?" he asked after a moment.

"I talked to Dad's attorney, Ted Delray. I believe you know him?"

A flush spread across the deputy's cheeks. "He's my father."

"He's handled all of Dad's legal affairs for years," she said. "I asked him about Dad's will and he said several years ago, Dad placed the ranch in a conservation easement. Do you know what that is?"

"Yes. It's a way to keep properties from being subdivided and sold off."

"Right. Dad left everything to me, except for a

small cash gift to the history museum, and I'm free to continue to operate the ranch, to hire someone to manage it for me or to sell it to someone who will keep it as a working ranch. There's nothing at all in the will about Darla or her son, Emmet. I told Darla that and she says there's another will—one that does give Emmet half the property."

"Did she show you this will?" Deputy Ellis asked.

"No. And I don't want to see it. I don't believe it exists. I told her to take it up with Ted."

"Is it possible she's right—is there another will?" Deputy Delray asked.

"Why would Dad make another will that Ted doesn't know about?" she asked. "Dad used him for everything. He even handled Dad's divorce from Darla." She shook her head. "She has to be bluffing."

"We can't help you with legal advice," Deputy Delray said. "But we're here if your unwanted visitors give you any trouble about leaving. Though we'd like to question them before you kick them out."

"Of course. Is that why you're here?" She put aside her agitation about the will to focus on him. "Or have you learned something new?"

He shook his head. "Nothing new. And we wanted to talk to you again, too." He moved to the kitchen table and pulled out a chair. "Why don't we sit and talk for a few minutes?"

She sat and they took the two chairs across from her. "How are you doing?" Deputy Delray asked, real concern in his expression.

"I'm still in shock," she said. "So much has happened so quickly. Right now I'm just powering through, and not quite believing Dad is gone."

"You don't have to do everything by yourself," he said. "Ask your friends for help."

She pressed her lips together, fighting for control. "I don't have many friends here," she said. "I've been away a long time."

"How long have you been back living on the ranch?" Deputy Ellis asked.

"Four weeks."

"How was that going—you and your father living together after you had both lived on your own so long?" Deputy Delray asked. "Or did you live on your own?"

"Dad and I got along well. For years after my mother died it was just the two of us, so we've always been close."

"So you didn't argue?" Deputy Ellis asked.

She shifted, then told herself not to squirm like a guilty child. "We were making it work," she said.

"We have a witness who says he heard you and your father arguing," Deputy Delray said. "The night before your father was killed."

A chill settled in the pit of her stomach. "We weren't fighting," she said. "Not really."

"The witness says the two of you were shouting," Deputy Ellis said.

She looked away, blinking back tears. "Dad and I both have tempers. But it was nothing, really."

"What was the argument about?" Deputy Delray asked.

"Dad thought I was wasting my life looking after him. He accused me of hiding here." Her father's words had stung, maybe because they were at least partly true.

"What were you hiding from?" Deputy Delray asked.

"I was fired from my teaching job at Hemphill University. At first, I thought I would stay here with Dad a couple of weeks, but that turned into a month."

"I'm sure being fired was painful," Deputy Delray said. He sounded more sympathetic than accusatory. Was he playing "good cop" or did he really care?

"Dad yelling at me about it was his way of getting me moving forward with my life again."

"But the two of you argued about it," Deputy Ellis persisted.

She nodded. "We argued. But it wasn't real anger. It was the kind of disagreement that two people who love each other have—they're not on the same page, but each of them is coming from a place of caring. I thought Dad needed me here and he believed I was wasting my talents hiding away here." She forced herself to meet his gaze. "I loved my father. I can't even imagine anything he could have done or said that would have made me angry enough to hurt him. I just…" She shook her head. "It wouldn't happen. He was my father. The only parent I'd had for years and years." She began to sob, unable to hold back the tears any longer.

"What time did you leave the house yesterday morning?" Ellis asked after a moment.

She sniffed and tried to focus on answering him. “About eight forty-five,” she said. “Dad is usually in for breakfast by eight, so when he hadn’t come in forty-five minutes later, I was worried. I tried calling his cell phone, but didn’t get an answer.” She frowned. “That isn’t so unusual, since there are a lot of places around here where the signal isn’t very good. But I was so worried I decided to go out and look for him. When I saw he hadn’t taken his truck, I was even more concerned.”

“Why was that?” Delray asked.

“If he was riding a horse or on a four-wheeler, he might have been thrown and hurt. Dad liked to think he was bulletproof, but he was almost seventy and he’s not as strong as he used to be. I thought if I moved back here I could make sure he ate better and got his rest and didn’t overdo it—but it was hard.” She almost smiled. “Dad could be very stubborn, but so could I. It’s why we sometimes clashed.”

“Where did you go looking for him?” Delray asked.

“I walked over to the horse barns first. The mare he usually rides was in her stall, so I thought that meant Dad was out on one of the four-wheelers. I knew he wouldn’t strike out on foot.”

Neither of them argued with that assumption. They had probably spent enough time around local ranchers and cowboys to know that was true.

“Where did you look for your father next?” Ellis asked.

“I drove over to Von King’s cabin, to ask if he had

seen Dad. But he wasn't there, so I figured maybe he and Dad had gone somewhere in Von's truck. That made me feel a little better, so I started back for the ranch house. But then I saw all the law enforcement vehicles over by the corrals and drove over to find out what was going on."

"What did you think when you saw the vehicles?" Ellis asked.

"I thought Dad had been in an accident," she said. "I was scared."

"You mentioned your father's temper," Delray said. "Do you know of anyone else he argued with recently?"

"No. I asked Ted that also and all he said was that a person didn't live to almost seventy without making enemies. I don't know if I agree with that, but someone disliked my father enough to kill him, didn't they?"

Deputy Delray looked at Deputy Ellis. "Do you have any more questions for Ms. Russell?"

"No." Deputy Ellis slid back his chair. "I've got a couple of calls I need to make, so I'll meet you outside in a bit."

He left the room and silence wrapped itself around Willow and the deputy. "We're not purposely being hard on you," Delray said after a long moment. "We have to gather as much information as possible, in order to find out who killed your father."

"I know." She gripped the edge of the table. "It's just hard, having strangers judge every part of your life. I'm not proud that my dad and I argued, but I'm not ashamed, either. He and I were a lot alike, and that meant we clashed. It didn't mean we didn't love each other." She shifted toward him. "I wish you could have known him, Deputy Delray. He could be stubborn and set in his ways, but he was also the first to help someone in need. Just like Von King—I wouldn't have hired him, but my dad wanted to give him a second chance. And if there was any kind of fundraiser in town for someone in need, everyone knew my dad was good for a generous donation."

"Could you call me Chris?" he asked. "It's what almost everyone else in the county calls me. I found out pretty quickly that most people don't stand on formality here."

"All right, Chris." Calling him by his last name always made her think of his father, anyway. "And you can call me Willow."

He nodded, a hint of a smile at the corners of his mouth and glinting in his eyes. "I met your father a couple of times, in my duties enforcing water laws," he said. "But he never broke those laws, so we only talked in passing. He welcomed me to the job when I first started, and he wished me luck. I never heard any of his neighbors say a bad word about him."

She nodded. "Which makes it even harder to understand who would have shot him. I don't even understand how someone could have gotten his gun away from him and used it to kill him. Not without a real struggle."

"The coroner says someone hit Sam in the back of the head and probably knocked him out."

"So they snuck up on him."

"Or he trusted the person enough to turn his back."

"That makes me feel even worse." She looked up at the ceiling, willing the tears not to fall. Her eyes and head ached from crying. "Though why it's easier for me to think he was killed by someone he hated than someone he liked—I mean, he's still gone, either way."

"I'm sorry," Chris said.

"That helps a little," she said. "Knowing other people hate that this happened and that some of them will miss him, too."

Chris stood. "I'd better go. But just remember—you and I are on the same side. We both want to find out the truth about what happened to your father."

She nodded. "Finding out who did this won't bring Dad back, but not knowing just adds to the loss. Does that make sense?"

"It makes a lot of sense." He rested his hand on her shoulder. The touch was brief, but reassuring. She still felt its warmth long after he had left her alone in the kitchen.

Chapter Six

Every encounter with Willow Russell unsettled Chris. He was confident he knew how to perform his job well, but that confidence faltered when it came to dealing with her. He told himself it was essential to put aside emotion and personal feelings to focus on facts in order to bring justice to Sam Russell's killer. That meant considering everyone who had come in contact with the man as a possible suspect. Willow Russell was probably closer to her father than anyone, she had no alibi for the time of his murder, she had admitted that she and her father had clashed, and as her father's only heir, she would inherit a lot of money and land worth even more. He had to look at her very closely and keep digging, yet when he was with her, he had a tough time believing she had hit her father over the head, then shot him at close range with a shotgun.

Maybe that just proved Chris didn't have what it took to be a criminal investigator. He knew as much as anyone in the state about water law, and never hesitated to enforce that law, even in the face of opposition from angry ranchers or irate homeowners. But murder was a very different story, with so much more at stake, both for the victim and the accused.

Willow had caught him off guard mentioning his father, and her connection to him. Of course, Ted Delray had lived and practiced law in this county a long time before Chris took the job with the sheriff's department. Chris had thought his moving closer to his parents would be a good thing, but he wasn't so sure. His father and he seldom saw eye to eye when it came to plans for Chris's future. Ted Delray had made it clear he thought his son was wasting his time in law enforcement.

Not unlike Willow's clashes with her father over her own plans for the future, he mused. Chris and his dad had certainly had their share of loud arguments on the subject—but that didn't mean they didn't love each other. If anything, that love made the disagreements all the more acute. He believed Willow when she said she could never be angry enough with her father to harm him.

But someone had been angry with Sam Russell, and Chris wanted to do his part to find that person. Because it was his job and he wanted to prove he had what it took to do the job. And maybe, he could admit, if only to himself, because he would like to be the one to bring a small measure of comfort to Willow Russell.

WHEN CHRIS AND Shane returned to the Russell ranch early Thursday morning, they found Willow waiting in the living room with Darla Russell and Emmet Caspar. "This is Deputy Delray and Deputy Ellis," Willow introduced them. "Darla and Emmet agreed to wait here until you had a chance to talk with them, then they're leaving."

"We're moving to a bed-and-breakfast in town," Darla said. "Much nicer and more conveniently located than here."

Willow nodded to the officers and left the room. Chris focused on Darla and her son. They stood close together, Darla's arms hugged tightly across her chest, fine lines fanning out from her heavily lipsticked mouth. She frowned at them.

"We appreciate you waiting to speak with us," Chris said, hoping to put her at ease.

"Do you have information about poor Sam?" she asked. "When will you release his body, so we can have a proper funeral? Do you know when they'll issue the death certificate? Have you found the person who did this?" She fired off the questions one after another, as if afraid she might lose her ability to speak at any moment.

"Sit down, Mrs. Russell." Shane gestured toward the sofa. "We'll do our best to answer your questions, and you can give us some more information about Mr. Russell."

The combination of Shane's leading-man good looks and charming warmth melted away much of Darla Russell's agitation. "Thank you, Deputy," she said. "It's nice to have someone acknowledge how much this has distressed me." She directed a sour look toward Chris. "Even though Sam and I were no longer married, we were still close. I want to help in any way I can."

Shane moved a chair from the dining table and set it up close to her. Chris sat in an armchair a little farther away, content to observe and let Shane take the lead.

"Let's start with getting some basic facts out of the way," Shane said. "Where were you between 5:00 and 7:30 a.m. Tuesday?"

"Oh, my." She put a hand to one cheek. "I'm sure I was asleep. I do require my beauty sleep, you know." She didn't exactly flutter her eyelashes, but somehow the gesture was implied.

"And where were you sleeping?" Shane asked.

She laughed. "Where do you think, Deputy? I was at home in my own bed."

"And where is home?" Shane asked.

"Albuquerque." She rattled off the address.

Shane looked to Emmet. "And what about you? Where were you Tuesday morning?"

"I was home." Emmet looked at his mother, as if for confirmation.

"Emmet lives with me," Darla said. "He's a great help to me."

"What kind of work do you do, Mr. Caspar?" Shane asked.

"Well, I—"

"Emmet is between jobs right now," Darla said. "It's something he and Willow have in common."

"When was the last time you spoke to Sam, Mrs. Russell?" Shane asked.

"You can call me Darla."

"When was the last time you spoke to Sam?"

She looked thoughtful. "I can't be absolutely positive, but I think it was about a week ago." She nodded. "Yes. We talked about Emmet and me coming to visit."

"Was that something you had done before?" Shane asked.

"Oh, yes. Sam and I were still good friends, and I still think of him as a father to Emmet."

Emmet's pained expression hinted that he didn't share this feeling, Chris thought.

"When you last spoke to Sam, was he upset or worried about anything?" Shane asked.

"He was worried about Willow," Darla said. "She moved home and didn't give any indication that she ever intended to leave. As if she expected Sam to support her for the rest of her life."

Chris shifted in his seat. He was tempted to point out that she appeared to be supporting her son, but Shane, probably wisely, didn't bring this up.

"Was anything else bothering him?" Shane asked. "Did he have any enemies you were aware of?"

"No. Sam was a wonderful man. He was generous and hardworking. Everyone thought very highly of him. We couldn't go anywhere around here where people didn't come over to talk to us or offer to buy us a drink." She laughed again, a high-pitched titter so out of keeping with her otherwise severe demeanor, it startled Chris. "It was like being married to a celebrity."

In his brief tenure on the job, Chris had heard many ranchers complain about their neighbors. So-and-so was greedy and Mr. Such-and-such was cheap. Mr. X cut corners and Mrs. Y thought she was better than everyone else. But he had never heard anything but admiration for Sam, who most often was described as hardworking, fair and honest.

"Chris, do you have any questions for Mrs. Russell and her son?" Shane asked.

"When did you learn of Sam's death?" Chris asked.

"Willow called me Tuesday night," she said. "I was upset that she waited so long. Poor Sam had been gone all day and I didn't know." She looked away, blinking rapidly.

"And what time did you arrive in Eagle Mountain yesterday?" Chris asked.

"I came straight to the sheriff's office," she said. "So—just before lunch?"

"You drove from Albuquerque?" Shane asked.

"That's right. I couldn't sleep, so we left very early."

"Why did you decide to come here?" Chris asked.

"I couldn't leave Willow to deal with this all by herself," she said. "Not that she's been appreciative of my efforts. In fact, she asked us to leave."

"Why did she do that?" Shane asked.

"I think she wants to hide the truth from me," Darla said.

"Why?" Shane asked. "What truth do you believe she's hiding?"

"The truth about what really happened to Sam. I believe she knows more than she's telling."

"Why would she want to hide that from you?" Chris asked.

"She was always jealous of me, Deputy. She couldn't accept that her father could love another woman. I blame her for destroying our marriage. Her jealousy and resentment put Sam in a terrible position."

"I thought Willow was already living on her own, out of state, when you and Sam married," Chris said.

"She called her father regularly and said terrible things about me," Darla said. "And when she visited she was very rude to me. After a while, it was too much for Sam. But I know he still loved me."

"Why do you believe Willow knows things about her father's death that she isn't telling anyone?" Shane asked.

"She was the only one here the morning he died, wasn't she?" Darla said. "She's in such a hurry to get us out of the house she must be hiding something. And she's already been on the phone to talk to Sam's lawyer about the will, as if she can't wait to get her hands on this place. I think that's suspicious, don't you?"

"How do you know she's talked to the lawyer?" Shane asked.

"She told me!" Darla drew herself up to her full

height. "If I were you, I'd take a much closer look at her."

"Anything else?" Shane looked at Chris, who shook his head. He didn't have anything more to say to this woman.

Darla stood and Emmet followed. "We'll be staying in Eagle Mountain if you need to talk to us again," she said. "*Someone* has to keep an eye on Willow."

They left the room. "I get the feeling there's no love lost between Willow Russell and her stepmother," Shane said. "After I left you two alone yesterday, did Willow say anything more about why she asked Darla and Emmet to leave?"

"I think it comes down to she doesn't like them and she doesn't want to share her home with them."

Shane nodded. "Mrs. Russell seems to think Willow had reason to murder her father," he said.

"If not always getting along with your parents is reason enough for murder, then it's a wonder so many parents live to an old age," Chris said.

Shane quirked one eyebrow, but didn't comment on this. "We should try to verify if Darla and Emmet were really in Albuquerque when they said they were," he said. "If they believe Emmet is due to inherit half the ranch, that could be a motive for murder. Especially if they're having financial troubles. She said Emmet is unemployed."

Chris nodded. "We'll do that."

"Speaking of unemployed, what kind of work did Willow do?" Shane asked.

"She was a professor of cultural anthropology."

"Hmmm. Probably not a lot of call for that in Eagle Mountain. So she might be hurting for money, too."

"She never mentioned Sam being stingy about giving her money if she needed it," Chris said. "And it doesn't seem the kind of thing to murder someone over."

"I think we might be surprised at how little it takes to push someone over the edge, but we need to see who else had a motive. Did Willow have any ideas?"

"No," Chris said. "We don't have much to go on so far."

He and Shane were walking out to the sheriff's department SUV when Chris's phone buzzed. The call was from the sheriff. "Where are you now?" Travis asked without preamble.

"We're just leaving the Russell ranch."

"Get over to Carstairs Park ASAP."

"Yes, sir," Chris said. "Where is Carstairs Park?"

"It's what they named that patch of greenspace at the far north end of Idlewilde Estates," Travis said. "There's a park there with some trails and a little pond. A fisherman spotted something in the water this morning. It's a side-by-side utility vehicle. I'm thinking it might belong to Sam Russell. You and Shane head over there and I'll meet you as soon as I can get away from this town council meeting."

"Yes, sir." Chris ended the call and looked at Shane, who was waiting by the SUV. "We need to head over to Idlewilde Estates," Chris said. "Carstairs Park."

"What's up?" Shane pulled open the passenger's door of the SUV.

"Somebody found a side-by-side in the pond." Chris took out his keys. "Travis thinks it might be Sam Russell's."

"Why does he think that?" Shane asked.

"He didn't say." Chris slid into the driver's seat and fastened the safety belt. "But if it is Sam's, how did it end up in Carstairs Park?"

"Maybe the same way his watch ended up less than a mile from there in that ditch," Shane said. "Maybe his killer put it there."

WILLOW WATCHED FROM the living room window as Darla and Emmet drove away. She had expected to feel great relief at their leaving, but the tension within her remained tightly coiled. She didn't have to look far for the reason: Chris's questions from the day before still disturbed her. Did he really believe she had killed her father? And if he and the other sheriff's deputies believed that, would they stop looking for the real killer?

Chris had asked if her father had any enemies. She couldn't think of anyone, but she hadn't lived at home in a long time before she moved back only a month ago. Maybe there was someone she didn't know about.

She moved from the living room to the spare bedroom her father had turned into an office. As she opened the door she had to stand for a moment, overcome by a wave of sadness. This room, more than any in the house, was Dad's domain. The scent of his aftershave lingered in every corner, mingled with the smoke from the cigars he thought she didn't know about. An empty coffee mug sat on the corner of his desk, a scene from a Frederic Remington painting printed on the white china. She had given him that mug for his birthday one year. The fact that he had been drinking out of it not long before he died almost undid her.

She pushed back the grief and focused on the task at hand. Why hadn't Chris asked to see this place, to learn more about her father as a way of learning more about his killer? It would be up to her to search these things for some clue as to who had hated her father enough to kill him. But where to start?

Darla's comments about Sam's supposed penchant for hiding money came back to her, so she moved to the room's closet, at the back of which sat a small fireproof safe. She found the combination where she remembered it—written on a piece of paper taped to the underside of the desk—and spun the safe's dial.

Inside the safe she found titles for her father's truck and several other ranch vehicles, bills of sale for livestock, paperwork for the ranch itself and envelopes of other papers she would go through later. A handgun that looked antique inside a wooden box, a velvet bag half-full of silver dimes. No cash.

She closed the door to the safe and sat back on her heels. Had Darla been right that Sam had hidden cash in other places around the ranch? But where? And more to the point—why? While her father had always been careful with money, he had never been a miser. And why would he want to hide his funds, instead of investing them or keeping them safe in the bank?

Still puzzling over this, she sat at the desk, the worn leather chair creaking in protest. The top of the desk was almost obscured with stockmen's magazines, auction flyers, old issues of the local paper, and the numerous receipts and bills that were part of a thriving cattle ranch. Despite the attempts of herself and others to persuade him to use a computer for his ranching business, Sam still kept everything on paper.

She opened the top drawer to her right, and was confronted with a jumble of cow-calf notebooks—little notebooks designed to fit in a shirt pocket, in which a cowboy could note which cow had calved and a brief description of the offspring—a simple way to keep track of the stock during one of the busiest times of the year. The books dated back ten years at least, the numbers—and sometimes names, too—of a generation of cows and calves that had borne the Double R brand.

The next drawer contained files—branding and vaccination records, ledgers recording ear tag numbers, veterinary bills and breeding records.

The top drawer on the left side of the desk yielded a heavy green ledger. She cleared a space in the desktop clutter and heaved the ledger onto it. The pages were inscribed in her father's neat hand. He had penmanship worthy of a draftsman. When she had commented on it once, he said it came from having a mother who was a schoolteacher. *Mother said a neat hand was a sign of a gentleman*, he had said. *She made me practice every afternoon before she'd let me out of the house to ride my horse. The only way I could get what I wanted was to get good enough for her to decide I didn't need to practice anymore. I guess it stuck with me.*

She scanned the columns of numbers and the careful notations—twenty-eight dollars paid for salt blocks, eight hundred received for a load of hay, twenty-four hundred paid for a trailer, eight thousand for a cutting horse, one thousand for a saddle. Her father had made note in these pages of every dime spent or received. She couldn't calculate how much money had passed through the ranch over the years, but she had long known her father was a wealthy man, though he valued the land and the livestock on it more than money in the bank or fancy possessions.

Finally, in the bottom left-hand drawer, she found the spiral-bound black datebook, identical to the ones her father had used for decades. He purchased a new one toward the end of each year at the local office supply. No fancy planners for him—a simple week-by-week calendar was enough.

She flipped through the weeks prior, where Sam had made careful note of appointments for haircuts, meetings of the local Cattleman's Association and lunch dates with friends. She reached this week.

There was no notation for Tuesday, the day he had died. In fact, the only appointment recorded for the whole week was for today—a four-o'clock "Meeting with A."

Who was A?

She closed the calendar and contemplated the disarray around her. Dad's whole life was in these records, if someone took the time to study them.

She turned her attention to the piles of papers in a shoebox on one corner of the desk. This must be Dad's version of an inbox—things that needed to be replied to or filed away. There were a couple of bills she probably needed to pay, an issue of a magazine he must have intended to read and some correspondence—a request for a reference from a cowboy who had once worked for him, a request for a donation for a local political campaign and a thank-you from a 4-H student whose cow her father had purchased at auction.

At the bottom of the box was a brown envelope. It contained a collection of letters—from formal, typewritten missives to notes scrawled in slanted, hurried script. Willow's stomach sank as she read through the letters. All of them were between her father and Adam Treadwell. She didn't know Treadwell, but in his letters he was identified as president of the Idlewilde Estates Homeowners' Association. Sam had written a series of increasingly agitated letters that accused the residents of Idlewilde of polluting the irrigation ditch that ran behind the development with runoff from their lawns and gardens. At first, Sam merely pointed this out and asked that people be educated about the ditch system and their need to refrain from using chemical fertilizers and poisons that could pollute the water—some of which could kill the hay or other crops, or sicken the livestock that made use of the water. Treadwell at first denied the problem, then claimed he had no authority to do anything about it, then threatened to take legal action if Sam didn't stop harassing him.

The last letter in the pile was handwritten, the letters large and slanted, embossed into the paper by the force of the writer's hand. It was unsigned, and without an envelope, but the message was clear enough. "Mind your own business or you'll be sorry."

Chapter Seven

Chris, Shane and Travis watched as a wrecker winched the side-by-side all-terrain vehicle out of the pond at Carstairs Park. Water ran in sheets from the dark green paint and sluiced over the vinyl seats. Mud slicked the tread of the tires and left a trail as the wrecker pulled the vehicle over a grassy berm and onto the gravel of the parking area.

"I don't see how it could have gotten over that berm unless someone deliberately ran it up there," Shane said as the ATV came to rest in front of them.

"We'll canvas the neighborhood," Travis said. "Maybe we'll find an early-morning jogger or dog walker who saw something."

"This is five miles by road from the place where Russell's body was found," Shane said.

"It's only about three miles if you follow the ditches," Chris said. "There's room alongside them for an ATV. That's what the ditch riders use to keep an eye on things." He gestured to the pond. "This is actually a wasteway from the ditch system, where they drain excess water."

"How far is this from the place where you found Sam's watch?" Travis asked.

"Less than a mile," Chris said.

A blue Toyota pickup pulled into the lot and parked on the other side of Travis's SUV. A man with dark hair just turning silver at the temples and the body of a football player going soft got out of the vehicle and hurried toward them. "What's going on here?" he demanded.

"Who are you?" Travis asked.

"Adam Treadwell. Idlewilde Estates Homeowners' Association president." He looked around, like a kid trying to take in everything at once. "What's happened?"

"What do you know about this ATV?" Travis nodded toward the dripping vehicle. "We just pulled it out of the pond here."

Treadwell stared at the ATV. "Did some kids run it in there or something?"

"Did you know Sam Russell?" Travis asked.

Treadwell frowned. "I knew him. I heard he died. Is it true somebody shot him?"

"Have you seen Sam around here recently?" Travis asked.

The lines on Treadwell's fleshy face deepened. "Sam was around here a lot lately."

"Oh?" Travis waited while the one word hung in the air.

Treadwell rubbed the back of his neck. "Not to speak ill of the dead, but that old man was a pain in my rear."

"In what way?" Travis asked.

"He didn't like the fact that we—this neighborhood—even existed. I guess he thought it should have all stayed hayfields or pasture or whatever. Anyway, he got it into his head that the people who lived here were poisoning the irrigation ditch with chemicals from their lawns and gardens. He kept writing letters, threatening to sue if we didn't stop. I tried to tell him I didn't have the authority to tell people what they could and couldn't do in their own yards, but he wouldn't believe me."

"You don't have covenants and things like that?" Chris asked. "Regulations on what size houses there can be and what color they are?"

Treadwell turned to him. "Of course. But there's nothing in there about lawn chemicals. And you can't just add regulations willy-nilly. It's a long process. I tried to tell Sam that, but he wouldn't listen. I mean, it's difficult enough to get people to understand why they can't water their lawns and gardens with the water running right by their property."

"Water law doesn't always make sense to people who are unfamiliar with it," Chris said. "If you like, I could come to a homeowners' meeting sometime and talk about the subject." He handed Treadwell a card. A big part of his job was educating people, and this seemed like a good opportunity.

"Thanks." Treadwell tucked the card in the pocket of his polo shirt. "Anyway, the last time I saw Sam was last week. He was in the park here, taking a water sample from this pond. I saw him and drove over to talk, but he wasn't having any of it."

"Where do you live, Mr. Treadwell?" Travis asked.

"Just there, across from the park." He pointed to a house across the road.

"Did you notice anyone in the park Tuesday morning, early?" Travis asked.

He shook his head. "I had to go to Junction early, so I was gone most of the day. I stopped in Eagle Mountain for dinner and someone told me about Sam." He rubbed the back of his neck again. "I mean, I didn't like the old guy, but I'm sorry he's dead." He turned and looked at the ATV. "Do you think this was Sam's?"

"We don't know yet," Travis said. "We're going to be canvassing the neighborhood, asking people if they saw anything suspicious," Travis said.

"Is that really necessary?" Treadwell asked. "I'm sure you won't learn anything useful and people here really value their privacy."

"It's necessary," Travis said.

Treadwell shrugged. "It probably was old man Russell. It would be just like him to dump the thing in our pond. He was that ornery. I mean, once he had made up his mind about something, there was no changing it. Do you have any idea who killed him?"

"We're still investigating," Travis said.

"Can you let me know what you find out about this?" Treadwell gestured toward the pond and the ATV.

"We'll be in touch," Travis said.

The sheriff turned away and Shane and Chris followed. Chris's phone had vibrated while they were talking, so before getting in his vehicle, he fished it out and checked his messages.

"This is Willow Russell. I've been looking through my father's papers. I've found something. I don't know if it means anything, but I think you should see it."

"That was Willow Russell," Chris told the sheriff. "She says she found something in her father's papers she thinks we should see."

"What did she find?" Shane asked.

"She didn't say."

"Stop by and see what it is." Travis checked his watch. "Shane, you can ride back to the office with me. We'll all meet at four to look at what we've got so far on this case."

"Yes, sir." Chris turned toward his cruiser.

"Chris?" Travis called after him.

"Yes, sir?"

"Ask Willow if one of their ATVs is missing."

"Yes, sir." Maybe this would be his chance to show Willow that the two of them could work together to find justice for her father. Chris didn't want to be her enemy, though when it came to Willow, maybe it was better right now if he didn't think too much about what he did want. A certain beautiful brunette might figure too prominently in his answer.

WILLOW'S BREATH CAME a little easier when she saw that Chris had come by himself. He was easier for her to talk to than the sheriff or the other deputies. Maybe he believed she was capable of murder, but at least he seemed to listen to her answers to the tough questions he asked.

She met him at the front door and ushered him into the living room. "Let's go into Dad's office," she said, and led the way.

He stopped in the doorway to take in the room. She tried to see it through his eyes—the battered wooden desk covered with papers and books, tall shelves crammed with more books, the steer skull on the wall, one of her father's old hats hanging from one horn. It was a worn, serviceable room, a good reflection of the man who had worked here. "We should have looked at this sooner," he said.

"I thought if Dad really did have an enemy, I might find out more here," she said. She sat in the desk chair. "Dad kept almost everything having to do with the ranch in this room, and the ranch was such a huge part of his life."

Chris came to stand across the desk from her. "What did you want to show me?" he asked.

"These." She handed him the stack of papers she'd placed in the center of the blotter. "That's a collection of correspondence between my father and a man named Adam Treadwell."

"The president of Idlewilde Estates Homeowners' Association," Chris said.

"Oh. Do you already know about this?" Maybe she hadn't given him enough credit for his investigative skills.

"We spoke to Mr. Treadwell this afternoon," he said. "He told us your father had complained to him about Idlewilde homeowners polluting the irrigation canal."

"Dad apparently kept copies of all his correspondence with Mr. Treadwell." She stood and moved around the desk and looked over his shoulder as he flipped through the papers. "Treadwell's responses are in there. You'll see Dad wasn't the only one with a temper."

Chris stopped and read the last note out loud. "'Mind your own business or you'll be sorry.'" He flipped the paper over to check the back, which was blank. "Did Treadwell write this, or your father?"

"I don't think that's Dad's handwriting," she said. She touched the edge of the paper. "This sounds like a threat to me."

"Treadwell could have been threatening a lawsuit," Chris said.

"Maybe. But don't you think it's worth looking into?"

"Yes." He tucked the papers back into the envelope. "I'll need to take these to the station, but I'll give you a receipt. We'll probably want to take a look at all of this, but is there anything else right now that struck you as odd or significant?"

"Dad had a note on his calendar for today—'Meeting with A.' But I don't know who A is. Could it be Adam Treadwell?"

"What about Tuesday? Any meetings scheduled then, especially first thing in the morning?"

"There's nothing recorded for that day." She handed him the calendar. "You can see for yourself."

"Did your father keep an inventory of property?" he asked. "We're trying to determine if one of the ranch ATVs is missing. I think that's most likely how Sam got to those corrals when he left here Tuesday morning."

"Yes." She moved back around the desk and opened the file drawer. She found the file labeled Vehicles and handed it to him. "All the registration papers and tax receipts for every vehicle on the ranch, including the ATVs, should be in there," she said. "And the titles to all the vehicles are in the safe, though I haven't looked through them all."

"Thanks. This should be helpful." He set both folders on the corner of the desk and took out a receipt book. "Is there anything else?"

"Just one thing," she said. "Maybe it's nothing, but then again…"

"Even something that seems small could be important," he said.

"Darla said my dad had a reputation for hiding money around the ranch. She said thousands of dollars. She said it was common knowledge—her hairdresser mentioned it to her. I looked in the safe and the desk for money and didn't find any. And I'd never heard anything like that before. But maybe Darla wasn't the only person who heard that rumor. Maybe someone else did and killed Dad for that money."

"It's something to consider," he said. "We'll see

about getting someone out here to go through your father's papers."

She held out her hands to indicate the office. "I know this looks like a mess, but Dad kept very good records, and they go back decades." She looked down at the open file drawer. "Somewhere in here there's probably a record of the car he bought me for my eighteenth birthday."

"Lucky you," he said. "I got a pen set and a new pair of jeans for my eighteenth birthday."

"This was an orange Vibe with primer on one fender. Not the cool ride of my dreams."

"Did you complain?"

She laughed. "I wouldn't have dared. I drove that car until I entered graduate school."

He laughed, too. Their eyes met, and she felt a zing of attraction that had her heart speeding up. She told herself to look away, but couldn't do it. The smile faded from his eyes, but he kept his gaze locked to hers. "How are you doing, really?" he asked.

"It's hard," she said. "But I'm stronger than I look. I'll get through this."

"I want to help," he said. "I know it's…awkward, sometimes. But don't let the fact that I wear a badge throw you. This job is all about helping, even if it doesn't seem that way."

She was finally able to look away. "Thank you," she said.

He put a hand on her shoulder, a brief, reassuring squeeze. "We're going to get to the bottom of this," he said. "We're going to find justice for your father, and for you."

She knew not every case was solved, and not every criminal was punished. But she wanted to believe Chris. Knowing he was working on her father's behalf made this horrible situation a tiny bit easier to bear.

"LET'S START WITH the timeline," Travis said, once the meeting of all available sheriff's department personnel convened Thursday afternoon. With a force as small as Rayford County's, there was no homicide division or even a team of detectives to handle a murder investigation. Every officer worked to solve the crime, with assistance as needed from the Colorado Bureau of Investigation.

Sergeant Gage Walker, the sheriff's brother, stood at the whiteboard at the front of the conference room and ran through the timeline he had filled in earlier. "The medical examiner ruled that Sam Russell died between five and seven thirty on Tuesday morning," Gage said. "Willow Russell and Von King both say Sam left his house between six and six thirty most mornings."

Gage indicated the next point on the timeline. "Willow Russell, Sam's daughter, states she came downstairs at seven thirty. Her father wasn't there, but that wasn't unusual. Sam usually came back to the house for breakfast about eight. When he hadn't returned by eight forty-five, and Willow was unable to reach him on his phone, she set out to look for him.

"Meanwhile, ditch rider Perry Webber finds Sam's body in the irrigation ditch by the shipping corrals at approximately 7:10 a.m.," Gage continued. "He drives to where he has a phone signal and contacts Chris." Gage pointed to Chris. "Over to you."

Chris consulted his notes, though the facts of that morning were etched in his memory. "I met up with Perry at the corrals at seven forty-five," he said. "I sent Perry to contact the sheriff. At nine fifteen, Willow Russell arrived and explained she had been searching for her father. She identified his body and returned to the ranch. Later that morning I got a call about a water violation in Idlewilde Estates and drove over to talk to the homeowner. I found a gold pocket watch in the ditch that Willow identified as her father's."

"This afternoon, we received a report of an ATV in the pond at Carstairs Park in Idlewilde Estates." The sheriff continued the narrative. "We've since identified this, using records provided by Willow Russell, as belonging to her father."

"So what do we think happened?" Gage asked. "How did Sam's watch and his ATV end up so far from his body?"

Chris had spent a lot of time pondering those questions. "Sam met up with his killer at the corral," he said. "When Sam's back was turned, the killer hit Sam in the back of the head with a rock or a shovel or some other heavy, flat object, then shot Sam with his own gun—which Willow and Von both agreed he usually carried with him on the ATV. The killer then took Sam's watch and drove the ATV along the trail that runs alongside the Daimler Ditch. He lost the watch behind the Howell property in Idlewilde Estates. Maybe he hit a bump, or maybe he threw the watch away on purpose."

"Maybe he realized taking something from a man you killed wasn't very smart," Deputy Dwight Prentice said.

"Maybe," Chris said. "In any case, the killer took the ATV and ran it into the pond at Carstairs Park."

"Then what?" Deputy Landry asked. "How does the killer get home? And what about the vehicle he used to get to the corrals? That's not an easy walk from anywhere."

"Maybe he—or she—had help," Deputy Jamie Douglas said. "Someone gave the killer a lift from Carstairs Park back to the corrals, or they drove the killer's vehicle away from the corrals and met up with him at the park."

"The neighbors who live near the park didn't report seeing anyone on an ATV in the area Tuesday morning," Travis said. "There are a couple of people we haven't made contact with yet, so we'll need to follow up with them."

"I took a call out at Idlewilde Estates about a Peeping Tom Tuesday morning," Jamie said.

"What time was that?" Travis asked.

"Right after I came on duty," she said. "So, about seven thirty."

"It could have been whoever dumped the ATV," Chris said.

Jamie consulted her notes. "The woman—Julie Breck, on Ash Drive—didn't mention an ATV. She said her peeper was a man dressed in dark clothes, on foot. He stood outside her bedroom window for several minutes watching her, then left. She was home alone and by the time she pulled on clothes and called us, he had been gone several minutes. I talked to her neighbors, but no one else saw anything. And definitely no ATV."

"Talk to them again," Travis said. "Someone may have seen something and not connected it."

"We should also ask about hitchhikers on County Road 361 that morning," Jamie said. "Someone might have given the killer a ride back to his car. He might have stashed it somewhere between the park and the ranch and walked to his meeting with Sam earlier that morning. We don't know if it was a planned meeting. Maybe the killer knew Sam would be at the corrals and ambushed him there."

"We'll put out a public appeal," Travis said. "What else?"

"Why get rid of the ATV at all?" Dwight asked.

No one had an answer for that. "Let's talk about motive," Gage said. "Who gained from Sam's death?"

"Willow Russell inherits the ranch," Shane said. "It's worth a lot of money and she's currently unemployed."

Shane was stating facts, but Chris had to clench his jaw to keep from blurting out a defense of Willow. Instead, he said, "Sam's ex-wife, Darla Russell, claims her son, Emmet Caspar, inherits half the estate. Though that may not be true. I'm waiting for Sam's attorney to return my call about the will."

"Von King and Darla Russell both said Willow Russell had recently argued with her father," Shane said. "Maybe one of those arguments turned violent."

"Why at the corrals, so early in the morning?" Jamie asked. "If they had a domestic disagreement, it seems like it would have happened at the ranch house."

"The ME said Sam died where his body was found," Travis said. "But Willow could have followed her father to the corrals that morning."

"So could have Von King," Chris said. "Or Darla or Emmet. None of them have a solid alibi for that morning."

"Anybody else have a motive to kill Sam?" Gage asked.

"Sam had feuded with a former neighbor, Bud Carstairs, who sold the property that became Idlewilde Estates," Shane said. "They were friends and haven't spoken in three years, as far as anyone I talked to knows."

"More recently, Sam argued with Adam Treadwell, the president of Idlewilde Estates Homeowners' Association," Chris said. "Judging from the correspondence Sam had saved, the exchange got pretty heated."

"Sam was upset because he believed Idlewilde Estates homeowners were polluting the irrigation ditch," Travis said. "Maybe dumping the ATV in the pond at the park—which is a wasteway for the irrigation system—was related to that."

"Any fingerprints or other evidence on the ATV?" Jamie asked.

"Sam's prints are all over it, but that's no surprise," Travis said. "Nothing else. The killer probably wore gloves."

"Darla Russell said there was a rumor in town that Sam had hidden a lot of cash around the ranch," Chris said. "Someone who heard that rumor might have killed Sam in an attempt to get that money."

"I'd heard that rumor," Travis said. "Not recently, but years ago, when I was in high school even. I'm surprised it's still circulating, but we'll add it to the list of possible motives." He glanced down at his notes. "The ditch rider didn't see anyone else out that morning, did he?"

"No," Chris said. "And we should go through Sam's records at the ranch. From what Willow showed me, he documented every dime he spent and every appointment he had. We might find something there."

"I've asked CBI for help with this," Travis said. "But the state is in the middle of a hiring freeze and they're shorthanded. It could be a few weeks before they can spare an investigator. I'd like to solve this before then."

"Someone saw something," Gage said. "There are too many people out and about that time of morning."

"Then let's hope we can find that person." Travis directed his gaze to each deputy in turn. "This murder has cast a shadow over the town," he said. "We need to find the killer and get rid of that shadow."

Chris thought of Willow, and the shadow grief had cast over her life. He couldn't remove that shadow, but he would do what he could to lighten it.

WILLOW DIDN'T RECOGNIZE the man who visited the ranch Friday morning. When she answered his knock on the front door, his expression was one of deep concern. "Willow, I am so, so sorry for your loss," he said. "I've been in shock ever since I heard."

He reached out, as if to take her hand, but she stepped back. "Have we met?" she asked. He was a good-looking man—tall and broad-shouldered with thick brown hair, close to her own age.

"I'm Trey Allerton," he said. "I'm leasing the sixty acres at the north end of this ranch. We met once when I stopped by to speak to your father."

Embarrassed that she had forgotten all about Trey Allerton, and annoyed that he took for granted that she would remember him from a single encounter that had lasted less than a minute, she flushed. "What can I do for you, Mr. Allerton?"

"Please, call me Trey." He flashed a smile that she felt to her core. It was a smile meant to dazzle, and it was effective. "May I come in?" he asked.

"Of course." She stepped aside to let him in.

He stood a fraction too close to her, and studied her intently. "Sam was such a great man," he said. "Losing him is a tragedy for everyone who knew him. My life won't be the same without him in it."

The familiar way he spoke about her father grated. Trey Allerton had leased that section of property less than two months ago, and her father hadn't mentioned him since. How could this man pretend they were close?

"Thank you for your condolences," she said. "Is there something else you needed to talk with me about?" Maybe there was a problem on the land he was leasing. She would need to handle those kinds of things in the future, or hire someone to take care of them for her.

"We need to discuss the terms of my lease," he said. "Not to intrude on your grief, but now that Sam is gone, the terms have changed."

"What do you mean, the terms have changed?"

"Let's sit down and I'll explain." He gestured toward the sofa. She wanted to resist, to announce she would remain standing. But she recognized the irrational pettiness of this, so mutely followed him and sat on the sofa.

He settled next to her—not touching, but too close for her comfort. "You may remember that I'm leasing that section of the ranch as the site for a youth camp I'm developing," Allerton said. "A place where disadvantaged young people can come to relax and rejuvenate in the great outdoors."

She nodded, not bothering to mention that her father had dismissed the idea as a pipe dream.

"Your father was one of my biggest supporters," Allerton continued. "His encouragement and enthusiasm for the project meant so much to me."

"My dad wasn't the enthusiastic type." She looked him in the eye and dared him to contradict her. Sam

Russell came from a family that believed outsized displays of any emotion were undignified and unnecessary.

"Well, he wasn't demonstrative, but he was definitely supportive," Allerton said. "He believed in our mission of helping young people and pledged to do all he could to help."

Light began to dawn. Allerton must be talking about money. Now that Sam was gone, he was hoping for a "donation" from Sam's estate. "You said the terms of your lease have changed now that my father is…gone," she said.

"Yes." He looked her up and down. "You take after your father, don't you? Direct and to the point."

"And your point is?"

The easy charm vanished, replaced by something harder. "Under the terms of the lease agreement I had with your father, in the event of his death it converted from a five-year lease to a forty-year contract at a cost to me of one dollar a year."

She couldn't hold back a gasp. "A dollar a year? My father was a better businessman than that."

"I'm sure Sam was a good businessman, but this was his way of showing support for what I intend to do with the land. And of course, he never expected to die so soon."

She stared at him, dumbfounded. "I'll need to speak to Dad's attorney about this." Why hadn't Ted mentioned this when they spoke Wednesday?

"Of course." Allerton stood. "I just wanted to give

you a heads-up in case you were anticipating the next lease payment."

He said a few more things about how wonderful and generous Sam had been as she walked him to the door, but she scarcely registered them. Her mind whirled as she tried to unite the version of her father Trey portrayed with the shrewd, stern, sometimes fractious man who had raised her.

As Allerton's truck was pulling away from the ranch house, she was already punching in Ted Delray's number. "This is Willow Russell," she told the woman who answered the phone. "I need to speak with Mr. Delray. Now."

Ted didn't keep her waiting. "Willow? Is something wrong?"

Everything, she thought. "I've just spoken to Trey Allerton," she said. "He claims his lease agreement with my father converted to a forty-year contract for one dollar a year when Dad died."

Silence on the other end of the line.

"Ted?"

He sighed. "I told Sam it was the dumbest thing he'd ever done, but you know how he was—when he made up his mind about something, he did it, no matter what anyone else thought."

"So you're saying it's true?"

"Yes," Ted said. "In Sam's defense, I think he did it as a kind of joke—a way of teasing Allerton. Sam never expected to die. He used to brag about how his father lived to be ninety-eight. And you know as well as I do that he was as healthy as someone twenty years younger."

"Yes, he was." And Sam would never have seen himself as a potential murder victim. But then again, who did? Ted's explanation made sense. Her father had seen through Trey Allerton's smooth charm and decided to bait him a little. He would give Allerton a sweet deal that made no sense from a business perspective, believing the youth ranch would fail long before Sam was gone from this world. "Did you tell the police about this?" she asked.

"No. Why should I?"

"Ted! Someone killed Dad. Maybe Allerton did it because he didn't want to make any more lease payments."

"I'll tell them," Ted said. "I'm supposed to call Chris today, anyway."

She wondered what Chris would make of Trey Allerton. They were both good-looking men, close in age, yet Chris had none of Allerton's smooth charm and salesman's persuasiveness.

She much preferred the deputy's competent calm. "Let me know what Deputy Delray says."

"There's actually something else you need to know," Ted said.

The reluctance dragging at every word made her stomach sink. "What is it?" she asked.

"Darla Russell and her son came to see me. They had just left when you called."

"And?"

"And she brought a copy of a will that leaves half the estate to her son and the other half to you."

"Is it a legitimate will?"

"That's what we need to ascertain. It's dated after the last will I drafted for Sam, but I need to do more digging."

The thought that she might end up sharing the Double R with Emmet *and* Trey Allerton sent a shudder through her. "What was Dad thinking?" she asked out loud.

"I don't think he was, Willow," Ted said.

He hadn't been thinking of her. The idea hurt—and it angered her, too. If Dad was here right now, they'd have a shouting match that would make their previous disagreements seem like ordinary conversation.

Chapter Eight

Adelaide Kinkaid, office manager, chief authority on community gossip and general mother hen of the Rayford County Sheriff's Department, had decided to take Chris under her wing. "I know you have a fancy law degree and you went through the academy—top honors, I hear—but that doesn't mean you know everything you need to know about policing in a small town," she told him when he reported for work Friday morning.

"Did someone complain about me?" He searched his memory. Had Mrs. Howell protested his cutting off the water to her garden? He definitely had the law on his side in that case.

"No one has complained," Adelaide said. "I just want you to have all the tools you need to succeed."

"Such as?" Was she going to tell him he needed to join the Elks Club or go to the high school football games?

"Wipe that smirk off your face, Deputy. I may look like an old lady to you, but I was married to a police detective for forty years. I know a thing or two about solving crimes, even if I don't do it myself."

Chris assumed a serious expression. "Yes, ma'am. What do you think I need to know?"

"First of all, this job requires a lot of hours, and even when you're not on the job, you carry the job around with you. Do you understand?"

"I think so," he said. "When people see me, they see the sheriff's deputy first."

"Exactly. Which can make it hard to have a personal life. The personal and professional bleed together." She waved her hand. "Don't stress about it."

"Don't?" Not that he had been.

"For instance, you might meet someone you're attracted to in the course of an investigation," she said.

"When I'm on the job, I need to put the job first," he said. "I need to remain professional."

"Well, of course," she said. "I'm taking for granted that you have enough smarts and class not to hit on a witness or a crime victim. I'm just saying it's okay to be human and have feelings. Things can work out."

"Is that how you met your husband?" he asked. "Were you a crime victim? Or maybe a suspect?"

She grinned. "I'll never tell. But yes, we met on an investigation. It happens all the time. In fact, I think every officer here met his or her significant other while conducting an investigation. It's almost like there's something in the water here."

"How is this going to help me be a better small-town cop?" he asked.

"It's going to help you remember that everything

and everyone around here is related in some way—and that includes you. You can try to remain aloof and distant, but it won't work. People have to trust you, and that means getting in there and being one of them."

He nodded. "Okay. But I don't think I'm being aloof and distant."

"I didn't say you were. Just don't think you have to be."

"Adelaide, what prompted this sudden concern?" he asked.

She pressed her lips together in a thin line. He kept silent, waiting. She folded her arms over her chest and frowned at him. "I know you're trained to look at the evidence and put together a logical story, which is all very well and good. But you need to look at the people involved in a case, as well."

He nodded. "Is there a particular person you think I need to take a closer look at?"

"Willow Russell."

This wasn't what he had expected. "What about Willow?" he asked.

"If you get to know her, you'll learn she's a very smart woman. She was valedictorian of her class here and went to college on a full scholarship. Some people around here fault her for going off and leaving Sam to run the ranch alone, but she would have been wasted on that ranch. Sam probably wouldn't have taken her help with anything, anyway."

He nodded. "Yes, I think Willow is very smart."

"So, she's far too sharp to kill someone by bashing him in the head and shooting him with a shotgun." Adelaide shuddered. "Her own father? If she had wanted the old man dead, she would have slipped poison into his food or arranged an accident around the ranch. I'll tell you something—the kind of violence that was done to Sam was over-the-top and heavy-handed. Clumsy, even. You need to look for someone with those characteristics. Get to know the people involved in this case and take that into consideration, along with the facts."

"That's good advice," Chris said. "I'll certainly keep it in mind."

She nodded and left him alone again. He booted up his computer and tried to focus on a report he was writing for the water board, but Adelaide's words kept replaying in his head. Her assessment of Willow—that she was smart, and that she wouldn't be the type to bash her father in the head, then shoot him in the chest—matched his own conclusions, but having his feelings confirmed flooded him with relief. He had worried that his definite attraction to Willow might have made him blind to something in her that pointed to her guilt.

She still had to remain on the list of suspects—she had gained the most financially from Sam's death, and she didn't have an alibi for the morning he died. But he would take Adelaide's advice and look for someone with a propensity toward, and perhaps even a history of, violence, as well as a reason to want Sam dead.

"Deputy?"

Adelaide was back in his doorway. Had she

thought of some other pearl of wisdom she needed to share? "Yes?"

"There's a woman here to see you. Actually, she wanted to see Shane, but he isn't in, and everyone else is busy, so you're it."

"What does she want?" he asked.

"She says she wants to talk. And she's very pretty, so consider yourself lucky." She winked, then turned and left before he could say anything else.

The woman Adelaide escorted to his desk was indeed pretty—a platinum blonde with blue eyes and a shapely figure. But the woman's lovely face was troubled. "I wanted to speak to Deputy Ellis," she said, and looked around the room, and the other two empty desks.

Chris stood. "He's not in now. I'm Deputy Chris Delray. Can I help you with something, miss?"

"I'm Courtney Baker." She perched on the edge of the chair in front of his desk, knees together, a worn leather shoulder bag balanced on her thighs.

"Is something troubling you, Ms. Baker?" he asked. "Is there something I can help with?"

"It's not me, really, it's my, uh, the man I live with. Trey Allerton. I think someone is trying to kill him."

This alarming statement both refreshed Chris's memory as to where he had heard her name before, and made him look over her shoulder toward the hallway. "Where is Mr. Allerton now?" he asked.

"He had a business meeting. He doesn't know I'm here. He keeps saying what's happened isn't really serious, but I don't think that's true."

Chris pulled a notepad toward him and picked up a pen. "Tell me what happened."

She took a deep breath, composing herself. "Yesterday morning, as Trey was leaving the trailer where we live, someone fired a couple of shots at him. I was standing on the front steps and the bullets whizzed right by Trey's head. I screamed and Trey dove to the ground. He shouted for me to go inside, so I did. A few minutes later, Trey came in and said everything was all right. I told him he needed to contact the sheriff, but he said it was just some stray bullets from a hunter and we would be foolish to make a big deal out of it."

Chris made notes on the pad. "And you live at the trailer on the Russell ranch, with Mr. Allerton?" he asked.

"Yes. We're staying in a mobile home, temporarily, until we can begin construction on the youth camp we're developing."

"When was this shooting, exactly?" he asked.

"Yesterday morning, about nine thirty."

"Could it have been stray shots from somewhere nearby?" he asked.

She shook her head. "That's never happened before, and I haven't heard any shots since. I think whoever was shooting was aiming for Trey. It was terrifying." She leaned forward, one hand on the desk. "I have a little girl—she's only three. She's with her aunt right now, but I'm afraid to let her play outside. What if the shooter comes back?"

"Could you tell where the shots were fired from?"

She shook her head.

"I can come out there and look around, but I doubt I'll find anything," he said.

"You probably won't. I looked after Trey had left, and he said he looked before he left, and neither of us saw anything. I was willing to accept that maybe it was an accident, and then this morning, something else happened."

"What was that?"

"Trey went out to his truck to go to work and when he opened the door, there was a snake curled up on the front seat. A big rattlesnake. He killed it with a big wrench, then threw it on the ground. I heard him yelling and came out."

"Maybe the snake crawled in through an open window?" Chris suggested.

She shook her head. "The windows were up. Someone put that snake in there. Trey thought so, too, though he lied and said what you did—that the snake crawled in there. Maybe he didn't want to frighten me, but I *am* frightened."

"Do you have any idea who would want to harm Mr. Allerton?" Chris asked.

"I don't know. And Trey says he doesn't know, either."

"I can talk to him, if you think that would help," Chris said.

"No. I just wanted you to know. In case something else happened." She stood. "Don't tell Trey I was here. It would only upset him."

"I'll keep your report on file," Chris said. "Let

me know if anything else happens, or if Mr. Allerton changes his mind about wanting to talk to us."

She nodded, but didn't move. "Is there something else?" he asked.

"I heard about Mr. Russell," she said. "I didn't know him well, but the few times I met him, he was very nice. I can't imagine who would have wanted to hurt him." Her eyes met his, wide and full of fear. "You don't think these threats against Trey could be the same person, do you?"

"Do you think the same person who killed Sam Russell is threatening Mr. Allerton?" Chris asked.

"I don't know." She hugged her purse to her chest. "It just seems so strange, that Mr. Russell was killed and then, two days later, someone tries to kill Trey. We live on the same ranch. It seems like the two things could be connected."

"We'll definitely look into that," Chris said. She was right—the timing and the location of the incidents did seem too much for coincidence.

"Thank you," she said.

She left, and passed the sheriff on his way into the office. "What did Courtney Baker want?" Travis asked.

"She reported that someone shot at Trey Allerton yesterday morning, and today there was a rattlesnake on the front seat of his truck."

"Hmmph."

"She doesn't know who or why, but she wondered if the incidents were related to Sam's death—maybe Sam's killer is going after Trey now."

"Someone who didn't like Sam leasing that section of the ranch to Allerton?" Travis asked.

"I haven't heard anyone complain about it," Chris said.

"What does Willow say about it?"

"She hasn't said anything."

"Maybe you should ask her."

"I will. But you said you knew Willow in school. Did she strike you as the type to go around taking pot shots at people or handling rattlesnakes?"

"Nope. But ask her, anyway. Maybe she knows someone else who isn't happy about the lease."

"I will." And he'd warn her to be careful. If the murderer had decided to target other people near the ranch, how long before he turned his attention to Sam's daughter?

WILLOW HAD STOPPED answering the house phone the day after her father died, weary of fielding condolence calls that inevitably morphed into attempts by curious friends and neighbors to glean more information about the horrible events. She still checked her mobile phone's screen when it rang, hoping to hear from Ted Delray. When she recognized Chris Delray's number on the screen, she debated letting the call go to voice mail. But she knew she needed to tell him about Trey Allerton's visit. And maybe the handsome deputy would have some good news for her for a change.

"Hello, Deputy," she answered.

"Hello, Willow." His low voice, with a hint of a

drawl, sent warmth curling through her. "How are you?"

How many times had she answered that question in the past few days? And had she really been honest with anyone? "This is all very hard," she said. "But I'm trying to keep it together."

"It's a lot for one person," he said. "Is there anything I can do to help?"

"Find whoever killed my father."

"I'm working on it. Can I stop by later this afternoon?"

She wished he was asking because he wanted to see her, but she knew better. "More questions?" she asked.

"I know it's tiresome, but you were closer to your father than anyone else. You know more about him and his activities."

"I don't mind the questions if they can really help."

"Could I come by about five thirty?"

"I'll be here." She ended the call and sat on the sofa, noticing the dust on the furniture and the clutter of old newspapers and magazines on the coffee table. She should probably clean, but she couldn't find the energy. She had tried, unsuccessfully, to talk her father into hiring someone to take care of the household for him, but he had argued that he didn't mind the clutter. *Besides, now that you're back home, you can do it,* he had said, which had led to another argument—one she had eventually lost. While he might have been able to live with the dirt, she couldn't. It wasn't the cleaning itself she minded so much, it was being forced into the role of unpaid household help.

She sighed and moved into the dining room, where she had set up her laptop. She logged on and checked on the half dozen applications she had made to various liberal arts colleges and universities around the country. Most of them hadn't bothered to reply, but her email did contain one response. She knew it was a rejection before she even opened it. If someone wanted to interview you for a job, they called first.

The rejection was from Mount Prince University. Her friend Cecilia had recommended her for the job, and she had had high hopes. She forwarded the rejection to Cecilia with a sad face emoji, then went to straighten the living room.

She was upstairs changing clothes when her phone rang. Cecilia's voice carried the soft accents of her Mexican birthplace, and a sharper accent of outrage. "I told them you were the best person for the job—that they would be so lucky to have you on staff," she said. "But someone heard about what happened at Hemphill and they got cold feet. I told the department head to his face that not hiring you because of that made it look as if they had something to hide. He had the nerve to tell me I didn't understand what it felt like to be a target."

"It's okay, Cece," Willow said. "It's not your fault. I really appreciate you putting in a good word for me."

"Someone will hire you. You're such a good teacher, they'd be crazy not to."

"Except I had the audacity to sue my former employer for sexual harassment. And lost."

"You didn't lose," Cece protested. "Rich Abrams resigned and the university paid you damages."

"Rich Abrams is still professor emeritus, still giving guest lectures, and my position was eliminated. They said it was part of restructuring, but we all know it was done to get rid of me." She took a deep breath, pushing back the bitterness.

"It isn't fair," Cece said. "I keep hoping you'll find a better position—one where you'll get the respect you deserve."

"I'm wondering if that's even possible."

"You can't give up."

"Sorry. I guess I'm all out of optimism right now."

"You've had a terrible time of it, I know," Cece said. "How's it going? You must have a lot to deal with at the ranch, settling your father's affairs and everything."

"I feel stuck until the sheriff's department finds whoever killed him, or wraps up their investigation. We can't even plan the funeral. And some stuff has come up with his will that is muddying the waters." She didn't feel like going into the details right now.

"Oh, honey, that is terrible!" Cece shifted to a teasing tone. "I don't suppose there's some big, handsome cowboy there at the ranch who can take your mind off your troubles?"

The image of Chris filled her mind. He wasn't exactly a cowboy, but he wore a Stetson and carried a gun, and had shoulders broad enough to bear any burden. “The only cowboy on the ranch right now is a fortysomething ex-con with questionable hygiene,” she said.

Cece laughed, as Willow had known she would. “Then I guess you’re going to have to get out more.” She sobered. “But seriously, I am so sorry about your dad. If there’s anything I can do to help, even if it’s just lend an ear when you need to vent, you call me. Anytime. And I’ll keep my ear out for word of any job openings.”

“Thanks. I appreciate it.”

She ended the call and turned to finish applying her makeup when the doorbell rang. She glanced at the bedside clock—four thirty. Had she heard Chris wrong? Or maybe he’d gotten away early.

Chapter Nine

It wasn't Chris at the door, but Von King. He didn't bother with a greeting. "What are you going to do about the south hayfield?" he asked.

Willow stared at him blankly.

"It's overdue to be cut," he said.

"Then cut it."

"I don't cut hay. You need to get someone in to do it."

His belligerent tone grated, but she bit back an angry retort. "Who does Dad use?" she asked.

"That's up to you to find out."

"And I'm asking you."

He didn't answer, merely looked away, his jaw set. She wanted to tell him to leave—her doorstep, and the ranch. But then she'd be stuck with no one to feed the horses and look after the fences—two things she was pretty sure he was keeping up with, because she'd seen him doing both chores only yesterday. She took a deep breath and reminded herself that a little ego stroking could go a long way. "Now that Dad is gone, I'm going to be relying on you for help," she said. "You're obviously more knowledgeable about the ranch than I am. Of course, I'll pay you for the extra time and effort."

"Yeah, whatever. Just get someone in to take care of that hay before it's ruined." Not waiting for an answer he turned away, muttering under his breath. She thought she heard something about him having to do everything himself.

She shut the door and locked it. Though Von had never threatened her, he made her uneasy, and he knew she was here by herself. Better to be safe. She went into her father's office and sat behind the desk. In her fog of grief, she had forgotten that the ranch didn't stop for anything. There were still animals to take care of and hay and water to manage. Time for a crash course in ranch management.

An hour later, she was still engrossed in her father's records when the doorbell sounded again. This time her caller was Chris. She let him in, then headed back to the office. "I'm working back here," she said. "Von King reminded me this afternoon that there are a lot of things that have to be done to keep the ranch running smoothly, so I'm trying to get on top of all of that. I'm so grateful Dad kept such good records."

"That's helpful," Chris said, following her into the office.

"He did everything on a schedule," she said. "And he wrote it all down. Thanks to him I was able to get a haying crew in day after tomorrow, and I know it's time to call the farrier to see to the horses."

"It sounds like you're doing a great job," he said.

"I'm doing the job." She sank into the chair. "I don't know how great it is." But the necessity of getting to work had shaken her out of her funk. It felt good to accomplish something.

"Do you think you'll stay here?" Chris asked.

"And run the ranch?" She shook her head. "I think the best thing would be to find someone else to run it for me—someone with experience. Or I could lease this property to another rancher."

"The way your father leased part of the property to Trey Allerton?"

"I'm talking about a real rancher, not a big talker who, as far as I can tell, hasn't done anything." She rubbed the tight place at the bridge of her nose. "Mr. Allerton came to see me this morning."

"What did he want?"

"Sit down. You might as well be comfortable."

"Long story?" He sat.

"Just complicated. The short version is that the contract Allerton talked my father into signing had a clause that changed the agreement if my father died while it was active. Now the lease is for forty years at only one dollar a year."

Chris looked as dumbfounded as she had been. "That's an unusual arrangement," he said.

"I confirmed it with Dad's attorney. He thinks Dad meant it as a tease, since the original agreement was for only five years and he didn't expect to die anytime soon. Allerton says Dad did it because he really believed in the project."

"But you don't believe that."

She guessed she wasn't hard to read. "Dad was sure Allerton's ranch would never host a single kid," she said. "He even put a clause in the contract that said any improvements Allerton made would become Dad's property when the agreement ended."

"So Allerton came here this morning to remind you of this change in the lease agreement?" he asked.

"Yes." She looked him in the eye. "Do you think Allerton could have killed Dad? So he wouldn't have to make any more lease payments?"

"I'll certainly look into it." He shifted, the chair creaking. "I actually stopped by to ask you about Allerton, or rather, about that lease. Was anyone upset about that agreement? Someone who wanted that land for themselves, or who had other objections?"

She shook her head. "Dad never mentioned anything like that."

"What did you think of the arrangement?" he asked.

She shrugged. "I left the ranch to Dad. If he wanted to lease out part of it, I didn't care. Knowing Dad, I would have said he saw it as an opportunity to make money on land he wasn't utilizing for anything else. Though it doesn't sound as if the agreement was entirely to his advantage. Why are you asking?"

"Trey Allerton's girlfriend says someone has threatened Allerton twice in the past few days. She wondered if it was related to your father's death."

"Do you think it is?" she asked.

"It seems a big coincidence—your father is murdered, then two days later someone fires shots at a man who is leasing part of the ranch. I'm looking for a connection." He leaned toward her, his expression grave. "You haven't been threatened in any way, have you?"

She caught her breath. "No! Why? Do you think I'm in danger?"

"No, no. Just—promise you'll be careful."

She sat back and told herself to keep calm. "I'll be fine."

"Have you found anything else interesting in your Dad's papers?" he asked.

"Do you mean anything that might point to his killer?" She shook her head. "I'm afraid not. Just notes about when to move the cows and calves to new pasture, when to sell the steers, which auction house to take them to and what trucking company to use to ship them." She sighed. "He and I never talked much about the ranch. I wasn't interested in taking it over, so I never asked, and he had done things on his own for so many years, he wasn't going to ask me for help. But now, it's as if he's looking over my shoulder, telling me everything I need to know." Her voice broke on the last words.

"It's nice to think he's still looking out for you," Chris said. He stood. "I'd better be going."

"Are you headed back to the sheriff's department?"

"No, I'm off duty now."

Suddenly, she was anxious not to be alone with her grief. "Would you like to stay for dinner?" Heat suffused her face as soon as she made the offer. Would he misinterpret her invitation? Was he going to tell her she was out of line—that he had a wife or girlfriend waiting for him?

"That would be great." He smiled. "It gets old, eating alone all the time."

She returned the smile and stood. "Let's go into the kitchen and see what we can find."

"It doesn't have to be fancy," he said. "I'm good with a sandwich, or eggs."

"One thing about living on a ranch," she said. "We always have beef." She opened the freezer and started sorting through the packages wrapped in white paper. "We've got T-bone, rib eye, porterhouse..."

He laughed. "Any of those would be good."

She pulled out two rib eyes and thrust them into his hands. "You're in charge of the grill, which is right out there." She pointed toward the back deck. "Though you'll need to thaw those first."

He hefted a steak in each hand. "I think I can handle it."

While he thawed the steaks under running water, she made a salad and sliced and pan-fried potatoes. He seasoned the thawed steaks with whatever he found in the cabinets, and by the time she had everything on the table, he was taking the meat from the grill. A few minutes later, dinner was ready.

"This looks and smells amazing," he said, as he took a seat across from her at the kitchen table. She'd opted for this cozier setting over the dark and formal dining room.

"What would you have eaten if you'd gone home?" she asked.

He cut into the steak. "My specialties are fried egg sandwiches, canned chili or frozen burritos. And there's always takeout."

"Your poor arteries."

"Don't tell me you eat like this every night." He popped a bite of steak into his mouth.

She laughed. "I eat a lot of salad, grilled chicken and canned soup."

"Then I'm glad I gave you an excuse to take out these steaks."

"Oh, I've eaten plenty of steak since I moved back home," she said. "As far as Dad was concerned, it wasn't dinner if it didn't include beef."

"I guess you had to make a lot of adjustments like that, moving back home after living on your own."

"Oh, yes," she said. "It wasn't anything I ever thought I'd do."

"Why did you do it?"

Was he asking as a cop, or as a man she was having dinner with? She decided she wanted to answer him, either way. "I wanted to get as far away from Connecticut and my old job as possible. Eagle Mountain fit the bill."

"What happened?" He sipped iced tea, watching her, then added, "You don't have to tell me if you don't want to."

So he was the man sharing dinner, she thought.

"I sued my department head for sexual harassment." The words came easily after so many months, though at the time she made her accusations she had struggled to detail all that had happened.

"That took guts," he said.

His assessment pleased her. "People who haven't been in that situation are sometimes quick to judge," she said. "But there are so many emotions surrounding harassment, or any time you're a victim, I guess. The first time the professor grabbed me in his office, I was in shock. I told myself I must have misread the situation. That sort of thing didn't happen to me. The next time, he threatened me. He told me no one would believe me and my career would be ruined if I tried to report him. I felt powerless. It took me a long time to get angry. Looking back, that still surprises me." She took a sip of water.

"What happened when you did complain?" he asked.

"The university had no choice but to listen. I made my accusations very public, and I'd kept a log of dates and times and situations. I refused to back down." She'd felt triumphant then, no longer powerless. But the mood hadn't lasted. "I ended up settling out of court and then the university eliminated my position. They said it was due to declining enrollment in the anthropology program, but I was the only person let go."

"What happened to the professor?"

"He agreed to retire, but did so with honors." She

didn't try to keep the bitterness from her voice. "He kept his title and his pension and everyone pretended nothing had happened, even though I'm sure I wasn't the first woman he harassed. I was just the first who objected publicly. I ended up being labeled a troublemaker."

Chris had laid down his knife and fork and stopped eating. "That's infuriating."

"It was," she said. "It is. But it made me tired of fighting, too. I love my job. I enjoy teaching. But I don't like the politics involved. And it didn't stop when I left Hemphill. I'm having a hard time finding a new position. Academia is a small, insular world, and most people know what happened. I'm still viewed by too many of them as a troublemaker who cut short the career of one of the most eminent scholars in anthropology today."

"I'm sorry," he said.

"Thank you." She cut off another bite of steak. "I thought being in a completely different environment would help me sort things out, so I came home."

"Did your father know what happened?" he asked.

She shook her head and finished chewing. "I was afraid if I told him, he would either be so enraged on my behalf that he'd call up the retired professor and threaten him, or he'd tell me it must have been my fault."

"He wouldn't have," Chris said.

"Dad had very old-fashioned views of women," she said. "Anyway, I only told him my position was cut and I needed to stay here until I found a new job."

"He was probably happy to have you home," Chris said.

"He was. But he worried about me. I guess he sensed something was wrong, even if he didn't know what it was." She shook her head. "Now I wonder if I was so wrapped up in my own problems that I missed something wrong in his life—some clue that something, or someone, wasn't right."

"It's possible your father had no idea anyone was out to get him," Chris said. "We haven't found anything so far that points to him having a specific enemy. Not of the intensity you think would lead to murder."

She studied him across the table. He had rolled up the sleeves of his khaki uniform shirt and unclipped the radio from his shoulder. A breeze had ruffled his hair and a hint of five-o'clock shadow darkened his jaw. He looked relaxed and perfectly at home in her kitchen—and incredibly sexy, too.

She shifted, unsettled by her attraction to him. She scarcely knew him, after all. And she wondered if he still thought of her as a suspect in her father's murder. She wasn't going to ask. She was tired of talking about it. "How did you end up as a sheriff's deputy in Eagle Mountain?" she asked instead.

"I got a law degree, then discovered I hated almost everything about being a lawyer," he said.

"That's an expensive revelation."

"It's more common than you might think. Anyway, my area of expertise was Colorado water law. I read a newspaper profile of a water cop in another county and thought it sounded like something I would enjoy and would be good at. I did a little more investigating, went through the state's law enforcement academy, then started applying to various jurisdictions."

"Did you take the job here because your parents are here?"

A pained look she well recognized crossed his face. "It's great being closer to my parents, but..."

"But it's hard to have them close enough to scrutinize your every move," she finished. "Believe me, I understand."

"They moved here after I graduated college, so I never lived here," he said. "But I'd visited and I knew it was a great place. It was too good an opportunity to pass up, even though I might have preferred to start out in the job a little farther removed from them."

"What is your job, exactly?" she asked.

"Water law in Colorado—who has rights to use the water that flows on the surface or is stored underground—is complicated. Just because you've got a stream or an irrigation ditch flowing through your property doesn't mean you're entitled to use that water. My job is to educate people about the law, and enforce it when necessary. I make sure the people who have a right to the water—who have paid for that right in many cases—get the water they need to grow crops or water livestock or whatever."

"But now you're investigating a murder."

He nodded. "Your father was found in a local irrigation ditch. I was the first law enforcement officer on the scene. And I'm a fully trained deputy, so while water law is my specialty, it's not the only thing I do. And it's not as if I'm investigating this case by myself. In a department as small as ours, everyone works a case like this. And we have help from the Colorado Bureau of Investigation. Don't think we're not taking this seriously and putting every resource into it."

"I don't think that." Their eyes met and she felt such a pull she could imagine leaning toward him, though she remained very still.

He was the first to turn his attention back to his steak. They were silent for the rest of the meal, though tension hummed between them. Surely, he was aware of it, too.

After they finished eating, he insisted on helping with the dishes. They stood side by side in the cramped space between the sink and the dishwasher, him passing her the scraped plates to load in the machine. She caught the scent of him, warm and masculine, beneath the lemony aroma of the dish soap, and was aware of the hard muscle of his arm as he brushed against her.

"Thanks for inviting me tonight," he said when the last dish was loaded and she was drying her hands on a kitchen towel. "This was really nice."

"It was." She turned toward him and their gazes met and held. This time, she did lean toward him. Would one kiss hurt anything? she wondered.

Before she could find out, a reflection in the window opposite startled her. "What's that?" she asked.

He turned to see what she was talking about, then swore under his breath. "What is it?" she asked again.

He had already turned, and was moving toward the door. "Call 911," he said. "I think it's a fire. A big one."

Chapter Ten

Chris felt the heat of the fire while they were still some distance away. Flames engulfed the wooden posts on either side of the entrance to the Russell ranch, bright orange against the dusky sky. Sparks had ignited a pinion tree near the entrance and the fire was quickly reducing the tree to a skeleton. He looked around for a hose. By the time the fire department got here from town, the flames would have spread across the land—and the wind was blowing toward the house.

"We need to get some water on this," he called to Willow, who was hurrying up the drive after him.

"This way!" She turned and ran, back down the drive and across to the equipment shed. He caught up with her in time to help her push back the big doors at the front of the shed. "We keep an ATV with a water tank and a battery-operated pump for putting out small brush fires," she said. She flicked on the overhead light and started toward the back corner of the shed. "There are some shovels on the wall over there, and a pile of feed sacks we can wet down and use to beat out sparks," she called over her shoulder.

He went to pull down the shovels and gathered up an armload of the sacks. Willow met him again at the open doors. "The ATV is gone," she said. She shook her head. "I'm going to run back to the house and see if I can call Von at his cabin."

Chris scanned the shed. A tractor shared space with a cultivator and other implements, including a wheelbarrow and a cement mixer. But no ATV. While Willow returned to the house, Chris ran with shovels and feed sacks toward the fire and began attacking any sparks that leaped from the main blaze.

Soon Willow was back at his side. "Von isn't answering the phone at his cabin," she said. "Help me fill some buckets and we'll haul water over here in the truck."

He helped her gather up half a dozen five-gallon buckets and started to fill them from the water hose, but she called after him, "We don't have time for that. Get the water from the horse trough."

A pair of horses ambled over to observe as he and Willow plunged buckets into the trough to fill them with water. Willow struggled to carry a full bucket to the truck while Chris followed with two. When they had all six buckets loaded, Willow jumped into the driver's seat and shifted the truck into gear.

Though less than ten minutes had passed, the fire had spread, consuming most of the entry posts and the archway over it. Willow soaked the feed sacks in water and began beating at embers on the edge of the fire, while Chris soaked the bigger flames with water from the buckets. Then he grabbed a shovel and began scooping up dirt and throwing it on other areas of the fire. The two of them worked furiously, not speaking, for the next thirty minutes. Once the wood of the entryway was consumed and they had extinguished the trees on either side of the drive, the fire died down. They beat out or smothered the last of the smoldering embers, then stood, catching their breaths and surveying the blackened area on either side of the drive.

"Someone did that deliberately," Willow said. "I could smell the diesel when we first got close."

"I smelled it, too." Chris pulled out his phone. "I'm going to call this in to the sheriff's dispatcher."

"It won't do any good," she said. "Whoever did it is long gone, and we don't have any neighbors to see. You and I were closest, and we didn't notice anything."

"I'm going to call this in," he said again. "Then I'll take some pictures and look around."

"Okay." She looked up at what remained of the ranch entrance. "My father had that put up when I was a little girl," she said. "A man had a business in town for a while that did sandblasted wooden signs and Dad commissioned that from him."

She sounded so calm, but he thought about how all of this must make her feel—she had come home because it was a place that was safe and familiar, and everything was unraveling around her. "Will you be okay while I go in and make the call?" he asked.

"I'll be fine." She didn't look at him, simply remained standing there, looking at the damage.

Inside, he called dispatch to report the vandalism. He was on his way to the front door when the house phone rang again. He answered and Travis said, "I heard the call from dispatch. What's going on?"

"Someone—no idea who—set fire to the wooden archway at the entrance to the Russell ranch," he said. "I helped Willow put out the fire. It was definitely deliberate—we could smell the diesel."

"Has she had any threats from anyone?" Travis asked.

"She says no."

"Could be kids out for trouble, or it could be something worse. I think I'll come out and take a look."

Chris joined Willow just as the first of two fire trucks arrived. The assistant fire chief, a fit sixty-something with short-cropped gray hair, walked toward them, studying the blackened area around the gate as he moved. "What happened?" he asked.

"Someone set fire to the entrance gate," she said. "We could smell the diesel."

"We spotted the flames about seven o'clock," Chris said. "I don't think it had been burning long when we got here."

The chief nodded. "We'll mop up, make sure all the sparks are out and collect any evidence of arson." He glanced at Chris, taking in the uniform. "Are you with the sheriff's department?"

"Deputy Chris Delray." Chris shook the chief's hand. "I called in a report of vandalism."

"Tom Reynolds. I'll let you know what we find." Reynolds returned to his crew.

The firemen were at work when a battered green pickup swung into the drive. Von King pulled alongside them and lowered the driver's-side window. "What happened here?" he asked.

"Where were you?" Willow asked. "Why didn't you answer my call?"

"Wasn't home." He looked past her, at the blackened remains of the entrance arch. "I told Sam he ought to replace that with iron, but he stuck with the wood. Iron wouldn't have burned like that."

"Where were you?" Chris asked.

"Out." Von's gaze met his, defiant and letting Chris know he wasn't going to get any more of an answer.

"Have you seen anyone hanging around lately who shouldn't be here?" Chris asked.

"Nope," Von said.

"Did you pass anyone on the way in here?"

"Nope."

"Where is the ATV with the water and firefighting equipment?" Willow asked.

"It's in the shed, where it always is," Von said.

"No, it isn't."

Von finally looked at her again. "Are you sure?"

"Yes, I'm sure."

His gaze slid away again. "Then I don't know what to tell you."

Willow turned to Chris. "Did you call the sheriff's office?"

“Yes. They’re sending someone.”

“I’ll be going,” Von said. Not waiting for a reply, he rolled up the window and backed up the truck.

“Do you know of an experienced cowboy looking for work?” Willow asked as they watched Von drive away.

“No. But I’ll keep my ears open.”

“Do. Because I don’t know how much longer I can stand having him around. So far he’s been the very definition of unhelpful.”

“I spoke to the sheriff,” Chris said. “He’s coming out to look at things.”

“There’s nothing for him to see,” she said. “There’s nothing for anyone to see. I think this is someone’s idea of a bad joke—maybe kids trying to make trouble somewhere remote where they know they’re unlikely to get caught.”

“Maybe. But we don’t see much of that kind of thing around here.”

“There’s always a first.” She looked down at her blackened hands. “I’m going inside to clean up,” she said. “Do you mind?”

“Go ahead. I’ll wait for the sheriff.”

While he waited, he prowled the area around the entrance and along the road several hundred yards in either direction, but he found nothing suspicious. He returned to the equipment shed and found ruts where he thought the firefighting ATV might have been parked, but no sign of what might have become of the machine. He washed his hands at a spigot beside the barn, and refilled the horse trough while the horses looked on.

Travis arrived in his sheriff's department SUV, his brother Gage in the passenger seat. Gage looked to where the entrance arch had been and whistled. "I remember when Sam had that made twenty-five years ago or so. It was a big, thick piece of oak. Not the kind of thing to burn that easily."

"I think someone soaked the base of the posts with diesel, then lit them," Chris said. "The first was really hot and going good by the time we got out here."

"You're lucky it didn't spread," Travis said. "We've had some wind."

Tom Reynolds joined them. "Evening, Sheriff, Gage," he said. He turned to Chris. "You're right—this was deliberately set. We've got an investigator in Junction we use for suspected arson and I could have him come out and do a more thorough inspection, but his services aren't cheap, and since the fire didn't spread..."

"I don't think an arson investigation is going to turn up much more than we'll find on our own," Travis said. "Thanks, Tom."

"We've done our best to make sure the fire won't reignite, but you should be alert for any hot spots that might flare up," Tom said. He looked at the sky. "It's supposed to be a calm night, so I don't anticipate you'll have any trouble."

They said goodbye and the fire crew departed.

When they were gone, Travis turned to Chris. "What do you think?"

Chris rubbed the back of his neck. "I don't know. It could just be kids, out to make trouble. But Willow said her dad kept an ATV outfitted to fight fires, and it's missing from the equipment shed. We ended up hauling buckets of water and beating out sparks with shovels."

"Did whoever set the fire steal the ATV?" Gage asked.

"Willow and I were in the kitchen, at the back of the house," Chris said. "I think we would have heard anyone in the equipment shed, especially if they started the ATV, or hauled it out on a trailer."

"So maybe they took it some other time," Gage said. "Or maybe there's no connection between the missing ATV and this fire."

"Maybe Sam sold the ATV and didn't tell Willow," Chris said.

"If Sam sold it, he'd have had another, better one in place first," Travis said. "He wasn't one to leave things to chance."

They walked the same path Chris had taken earlier, around the gate and along the roadside in either direction, scanning the ground for a tire print or cigarette butt or cap from a diesel can, anything that might be tied to their arsonist. But they found nothing but scorched earth and weeds.

"Was there anyone else on the ranch when this happened?" Travis asked when they were back in the drive, standing beneath where the archway had once been.

"Von King lives in a cabin not far from the corrals," Chris said. "When Willow called him, he didn't answer. He drove up after the fire was out and asked what happened. When he found out you were on your way, he left."

"I've been doing some digging," Gage said. "Von King is really Leroy Paige, from Oklahoma. He has a record for armed robbery, car theft and a few other minor crimes. But he's kept his nose clean since he got out of prison last year, as far as we know."

"Can't see why he'd do something like this," Travis said. "This is petty."

"Do you think it was meant as a threat?" Chris asked. "To frighten Willow?"

"Is she frightened?" Travis asked.

"She's hard to read," Chris admitted. Willow had seemed more annoyed than worried, but she struck him as someone who kept her emotions under wraps.

"Someone killed Sam on the ranch," Travis said. "Courtney Baker says someone's been threatening Trey Allerton, who lives on another part of the ranch. And now this."

"Maybe the target isn't any one person, but the ranch," Gage said. "Maybe someone is trying to run off everyone here."

"But why?" Chris asked. "The ranch isn't for sale, so it's not as if the people here are standing in the way of anyone or anything. The whole place is in a conservation easement, so it's not as if running off the owners would result in it going on the market."

"Maybe whoever is doing this doesn't know that," Travis said.

"Who would gain if Willow and Allerton left the place?" Gage asked.

"Darla Russell's son, Emmet Caspar, has a will that leaves him half the place," Chris said. "Maybe he thinks if he can scare off Willow, he can get her half at a bargain price."

"Let's take a harder look at the two of them," Travis said.

Willow emerged from the house. She had changed from jeans and a blouse into a cotton dress with a long skirt and ruffled sleeves. She'd braided her hair and it hung over one shoulder. When she came to stand by Chris, he smelled the floral fragrance of her soap. "Did you find anything?" she asked, addressing her question to no one in particular.

"Nothing significant," Travis said. "Have you seen anyone around here lately who shouldn't have been here? Anyone who didn't belong?"

"I haven't seen anyone but a few neighbors who came to offer their condolences," she said. "And most of them I've known all my life. They wouldn't have any reason to do something like this."

"Where are your stepmother and her son right now?" Gage asked.

"I don't really know. They said something about

staying in town, or they might have gone back to Albuquerque. Why? Do you think they would do this?"

"I'd feel better if I knew where they were," Chris said.

She shook her head. "This is stupid enough for Emmet to have come up with it," Willow said. "My dad used to talk about how dumb and lazy he was. Which is why I can't wrap my head around Dad leaving even part of the ranch to him."

"Do you think the will Darla gave your lawyer is a fake?" Chris asked.

"I think it has to be," she said. "Though proving so may be tough."

Travis and Gage took pictures and measurements, then left. Chris lingered. "I'm worried about you, here by yourself," he told Willow.

"I'll be fine," she said. She motioned toward the burned area. "This is just stupid. I can't even take it seriously as a threat."

"Still, after what happened to your father... I'm not trying to frighten you, but you should be careful."

"I promise, I'll be careful. And I'll call you if anything else happens."

"Call me," he said. "Call 911, too."

"I will." She put her hand on his arm. "Don't worry about me. I'm used to standing up to people who threaten me—I don't run."

He knew Willow didn't lack courage. But standing up to her department head had cost her her job—what if standing up to her current foe cost her her life?

Chapter Eleven

After a restless night, Willow woke determined to focus on the work that needed to be done. She started by walking up the drive to the burned area and assessing the damage. The acrid odor of burned wood lingered in the area, and ashes crunched underfoot. When Von swung his truck into the drive, she flagged him down. “I need you to clean this up this morning,” she said. “The charred fence posts need to be replaced, and cut down the burned trees on either side of the drive.”

She halfway expected him to argue with her, but he remained mute, so she charged ahead. “The farrier is coming at one o’clock to see to the horses, and the haying crew starts tomorrow.” If she had expected him to be impressed, he didn’t show it.

She returned to the house and spent the rest of the morning going through her dad’s calendar, making note of upcoming tasks she would need to see to. She wondered if one of the neighboring ranchers would be willing to help her evaluate the stock and decide which should be sold and which kept. She’d have to think about that. After her father died, several neighbors had extended offers of help, but how serious had they been about that?

She was finishing up lunch when she heard the crunch of tires on gravel. Expecting the farrier, she glanced out the window, only to see a familiar white sedan. The car stopped and Darla and Emmet climbed out.

Willow charged outside to meet them. "What are you doing here?" she asked.

"We talked to the lawyer and showed him the will," Darla said. "Half the ranch is going to be Emmet's, so we're moving back in."

"You can't make us leave," Emmet said, and heaved a large suitcase out of the trunk of the car.

Willow returned to the house, anger choking her. She punched in Chris's number. "Willow," he answered. "How are you doing?"

"Darla and Emmet just showed up," she said. "They're moving back in. Darla says since the ranch is going to be half Emmet's, I can't make them leave. That can't be right, can it?"

"My specialty is water law, not estate law," he said. "You should probably call my dad."

"I'm asking you," she said. She was annoyed with Ted for concealing so much from her already.

"If the will hasn't been probated, you could cite them for trespassing, I'd think," he said. "Though it might make things more difficult later, if the will does turn out to be legitimate."

"I can't stand them," she said. "Maybe you should

come out here and question them about the fire last night."

"I'll do that," he said. "I have some things to take care of here first. Will you be all right until I can get there?"

"I'll be fine," she said. She already felt foolish, calling him so impulsively. "It's not as if those two are going to hurt me or anything."

"I promise I'll be there as soon as I can."

She returned to her father's office and tried to ignore the sounds of Darla and Emmet going in and out of the house. But she couldn't ignore it when Darla knocked on the office door and called, "Willow! There's a very good-looking man here to see you."

Her heart leaped. Chris must have gotten away from the office much sooner than he had thought. She smoothed her hair and hurried out to greet him.

Only to be met by a smiling Trey Allerton. "Willow!" He greeted her like an old friend, and pulled her close in a crushing hug.

She pushed him away and stepped back. "What do you need, Mr. Allerton?" she asked.

"Trey was just telling me that he's building a ranch for young people just down the road from here." Darla hovered at Trey's elbow, giving him her biggest smile. "That's so admirable."

"It's the least I can do," he said. "There's so much need in the world." He turned back to Willow. "And right now, I need to borrow a tractor. Just for a few hours."

"No, I can't lend you a tractor," she said.

"But why not?" Darla asked. "You don't even know why he needs it."

It didn't matter why he needed it, she didn't want to lend him anything. He smiled at Darla, who flushed pink and all but simpered. "Someone dumped a wrecked ATV and it's blocked my driveway," he said. "I need to pull it out of the way."

"Pull it out of the way with your truck," Willow said. "I can lend you some chain, if you need me to."

"A tractor would be easier," he said.

"Where did the ATV come from?" she asked. "Who dumped it there?"

"I don't know," he said.

"When did this happen?" she asked.

"Sometime last night. It was there when we woke up this morning. I had to take down part of the fence to get out of the driveway, then drive through the ditch."

"What kind of ATV?" she asked, a growing feeling of dread overtaking her.

"A big one. With a water tank or something like that on the back."

"Did you report this to the sheriff?" she asked.

"I didn't see any need to do that."

"I think that might be one of the ranch's ATVs," she said. "It's missing from the equipment shed."

"Huh," Trey said. "About the tractor..."

"I'm not lending it to you," she said.

"Of course you can borrow the tractor," Darla said. She turned to Willow. "Half of that tractor belongs to Emmet and I know he won't mind if Trey borrows it for a little while."

"Until my father's will is probated, as executor of the estate, I have final say in what happens here," she said. She wasn't entirely sure that was true, but it sounded good, and it wasn't as if Darla had a legal degree.

Darla made a face and started to argue, but Trey cut her off. "Where's Von? Can I at least ask him to come and help me?"

"He's supposed to be cleaning up around the entrance," she said. "Didn't you see him when you drove in?"

"No," Trey said. "I did notice the archway is gone. What happened?"

"Yes, what happened?" Darla said. "Don't tell me you're making changes to the ranch already. That can't be legal, executor or not."

"Someone set fire to the archway last night," Willow said. "Do either of you know anything about that?"

Trey shook his head. "I'll go see if I can find Von."

"I need to talk to you about where we'll be staying," Darla said. "I want to change to a better room."

"Which room?" Willow asked.

"The master bedroom isn't being used, and after all, it used to be mine."

"You're not moving into Dad's room," Willow said.

"I don't see why not. I—"

As far as Willow was concerned, this wasn't open for discussion. She shook her head and walked past them, toward the door.

"Where are you going?" Darla called after her.

"Away," she said. She had had enough of all of them. She had to get out of here before she said or did something she would regret.

"What if something comes up?" Darla called after her.

"Deal with it," Willow said.

CHRIS WAS SURPRISED to see Willow striding down the sidewalk toward him when he stepped out of the Cake Walk Café after a late lunch. Despite her diminutive stature, she made a striking picture, with her long braid of dark hair over one shoulder and her curvy figure. He hurried to meet her. "I was just headed out to the ranch," he said.

"You don't need to rush," she said. "Darla has dug in her heels and I don't think she intends to go anywhere anytime soon. And where she goes, Emmet follows."

He fell into step beside her as she continued down the sidewalk. "What brings you to town?" he asked.

"I came to buy new locks for the door of my dad's office and my bedroom door," she said. "I don't trust Darla or Emmet not to snoop in there the minute my back is turned. She's probably in there right now."

"I can ask her to leave," he said. "Tell her you have the option of pressing charges."

"No, don't do that," she said. She glanced at him.

"I've decided I'm better off keeping them both where I can know what they're up to. You know the old saying—keep your friends close, and your enemies closer."

He would have laughed, but she looked too distressed for mirth. "Did something in particular happen this morning that has you so upset?" he asked.

"Everything," she said. "In addition to Darla and Emmet moving back in, Von has disappeared. When he showed up for work this morning, I asked him to clean up after the fire, to replace the burned fence posts and cut down the trees, and he left without doing anything or saying anything. And then Trey Allerton came by wanting to borrow a tractor. When I wouldn't lend him one, he asked if he could have Von help him for a while." She stopped and faced Chris. "Trey says someone dumped a wrecked ATV in his driveway last night, blocking in his truck. He had to take down the fence and drive through the ditch to get out. He said it was a big ATV with a water tank on the back."

"Like your missing ATV," Chris said.

"Yes. I'm betting it's the ranch's, and whoever set the fire put it down there. But I don't know why. It doesn't even feel like a threat, just annoying." She started walking again. "Anyway, I'm headed to the newspaper office to run an ad for someone to help me on the ranch. Then I'm going to fire Von. My dad may have liked him for some unknown reason, but I never want to see him again."

"Fair enough," he said. "Why don't I go with you, and I'll follow you back to the ranch."

"Okay." She took a deep breath and she visibly relaxed her shoulders. "What have you been doing this morning?"

"It was ridiculous, really," he said. "I had to separate two ranchers who were having a fistfight over whose turn it was to draw down from an irrigation ditch that divides their property."

"I guess people get very passionate about things like that," she said.

"There's a fine line between passion and rage sometimes," he said. "Most of the time just talking to the people resolves things, but sometimes I have to get out the handcuffs."

"I don't think you'll have to go that far with Darla and Emmet, but who knows," she said. "I've given up trying to figure people out."

"Did you take a look at the ATV at Trey's place to see if it was yours?" he asked.

She shook her head. "I didn't have the heart. But we can drive down there when you're done questioning Darla. It didn't sound to me as if it was going anywhere anytime soon."

They entered the newspaper office and the woman at the desk gave Willow an ad form to fill out. Willow completed the form, paid for the ad, and she and Chris left again. "I need to stop by the office and get my cruiser," Chris said. "Then I'll drive you to your car."

But when they entered the office, Adelaide greeted

him. "I've been looking for you," she said. "Both of you, actually."

"What's up?" Chris asked.

"You need to get back out to the ranch," Adelaide said. "Darla Russell just called. She was hysterical, but she said something about a fight."

Chapter Twelve

Chris pulled his cruiser in behind another sheriff's department SUV in front of the ranch house. Willow drove past him to park in front of the garage. As they all exited their vehicles, Darla Russell ran toward them. "They're in the machine shed," she said. "You have to stop them before they kill each other."

Chris, along with Gage and Deputy Dwight Prentice, headed toward the machine shed. Willow stayed back with Darla, the two in earnest conversation. Emmet met the deputies at the door of the shed. "What's going on?" Gage asked.

"It's just a fight," he said. "Mom didn't really need to call you."

Chris and Dwight moved past him, to the rear stall where Trey Allerton and Von King were flailing at each other. Von had Trey in a headlock and was repeatedly punching the side of his head, but as the two deputies reached the combatants, Trey broke the hold and landed a solid blow to Von's stomach that doubled the older man over.

"Break it up, you two!" Dwight wrapped his arms

around Trey and held him firm, while Chris dragged Von to the opposite corner.

"What was all that about?" Chris asked.

Von straightened and wiped the back of his hand across his nose, then pulled out a bandanna and began dabbing at his bleeding lip. "When I do a job for a man, I expect to be paid," he said.

"You'll get your money when you finish the job," Trey shouted. Dwight had released his hold on the man and he stood leaning against the wall.

"Who threw the first punch?" Gage asked.

"He did!" Trey and Von spoke at once, each pointing to the other.

Willow and Darla joined them. "I heard shouting and Emmet and I came out here and those two were trying to kill each other," Darla said.

"If I wanted him dead, he wouldn't be standing there," Von said.

"We're not done yet," Trey said.

"Both of you shut up," Gage said. "And stay away from each other or I'll haul you both in for assault."

The two men looked sullen, but said nothing else.

"Go home and cool off," Gage said. "Both of you."

Von was the first to leave. He sent a last malevolent look to Trey, then headed out of the shed. As he passed Willow, she called to him, "Von, wait!"

He stopped and looked at her, his expression sullen.

"You need to get your things and leave," she said.

"What?"

"You're fired," she said.

He drew himself up to his full height. "You can't fire me."

"I can and I am. Get your things and go. If you leave an address, I'll mail your final check in a couple of days."

"This place will fall apart without me," he said.

"I doubt that."

"You'll be sorry," he said.

Chris moved up behind Von. "If you cause any trouble for Ms. Russell, I'll arrest you," he said. "If you bother her in any way, you'll be in jail. Is that clear?"

Von grunted and moved on.

"I'll make sure he leaves without making trouble." Gage joined Chris and Willow.

"Aren't you going to arrest them?" Darla asked.

"Neither of them wants to press charges," Gage said. "Neither of them is badly injured and I don't see any property damage. Whatever the fight was about, let's hope they've got it out of their system." He turned to Willow. "Do you have any idea what the fight was about?"

She shook her head. "I know that Trey sometimes hires Von to work around his place. Maybe it's something to do with that."

Gage turned to Chris. "You make sure Trey goes to his place and stays there."

"Yes, sir," Chris said.

Gage and Dwight went after Von and Chris moved closer to Willow. "Will you be all right?" he asked.

"Can you handle things here until you can hire someone?"

"I will." She turned to Darla and Emmet. "You two are going to have to pitch in to look after the livestock and keep the ranch going," she said.

Darla looked startled. "We don't know anything about ranching."

"Then you're going to learn. As long as you two are staying here, you might as well earn your keep." She turned and strode back toward the house, her long braid of hair swinging behind her. Chris grinned. Some people might have crumpled under the strain of all Willow had been through, but the adversity only seemed to make her stronger.

Trey Allerton limped past Chris. "Are you okay?" Chris asked.

Trey put a hand to his side. "My ribs are a little bruised, I think, but I'll be okay. I figure Von is hurting at least as bad."

"I'm going to follow you back to your trailer," Chris said.

Trey didn't even try to object. Chris waited while he climbed into his truck and started the engine, then got into his cruiser and followed him on the short drive to the trailer.

The first thing he saw as he approached the mobile home was the busted ATV and trailer with a water tank straddled across the drive, and a section of fence lying in the ditch. Trey drove past the driveway, then through the ditch into the bare dirt area in front of the trailer.

Chris parked on the road and walked over to the ATV. "Willow Russell is missing an ATV and trailer like this," he said.

"Then she's welcome to come get it," Trey said. "It's in my way."

"How did it end up here?" Chris asked.

"Someone dumped it here."

"Any idea who?"

Trey shoved his hands into the front pockets of his jeans. "I have ideas, but no proof."

"Tell me and we'll see about getting proof."

Trey waved his hand toward the ATV. "Just get it out of here. That's all I care about."

"Do you think Von did this?" He would have had access to the ATV in the machine shed.

"I don't care if he did or if he didn't." Trey looked sullen, all of his easy charm vanished.

"Tell me what you and Von were fighting about," Chris said.

"I hired him to do a job for me, but he only did half of it. I told him I wouldn't pay him until he finished the work and he pitched a fit."

"What was the job?"

Trey looked around them. "Just some work around here. You can see this place needs a lot of work." He pointed behind the trailer. "All of that needs to be cleared, so we can build cabins and a lodge for the campers. We need new fencing and a front gate, some corrals and stables—all kinds of stuff."

As far as Chris could determine, no one had made

a start on any of these projects. "It sounds to me like you need a whole crew of people to do all that."

"I do. But that takes money. I spend my days talking to people, persuading them to invest in the project. I'm make progress, even if you don't see it yet."

"Do you think Von King is the person who shot at you?"

"How did you know about that?"

"We had a report."

Trey scowled. "I told Courtney not to involve you people."

"Do you think Von fired those shots?" Chris asked.

"It was just hunters."

"And the snake?"

Trey looked at Chris, his expression bland. "What snake?"

"Your girlfriend told us someone put a snake in your truck."

"I don't know what you're talking about."

Chris looked toward the trailer. "Should I go inside and ask her?"

"She's not there."

"Where is she?"

Trey shrugged. "Visiting her sister? Shopping? I don't know."

"I understand Sam Russell's death put you in a better financial position," Chris said.

"You mean no more quarterly lease payments, I guess," Trey said. "That will be more money we can put to use to benefit the kids. I was touched Sam would do such a thing."

"You knew that provision was in your lease agreement," Chris said. "It didn't come as a surprise."

"No. I was still sorry Sam was killed."

"You don't know anything about his murder, do you?"

Another direct, cold look. "I didn't kill Sam Russell," he said. "But I hope you find who did. And I need to go inside and clean up now. I have a meeting this afternoon."

Chris looked back at the ATV. "I'll need to go in and use your phone to call this in." He had no cell service here.

"I don't have one," Trey said. "When I want to talk to someone, I do it in person."

"That's not very convenient," Chris said.

"It has its benefits. And its drawbacks. If I'd called Von instead of going over to the ranch to speak to him, maybe our tempers wouldn't have got the better of us."

"There was a fire at the ranch last night," Chris said. "Someone torched the entrance gate. Do you know anything about that?"

Trey shook his head. "I was here last night. With Courtney and her daughter." He touched the split at the corner of his eye. "Something funny you might want to know about, though."

"What's that?" Chris asked.

"When I went into the machine shed, looking for Von, he wasn't there. But Darla's boy, Emmet, was."

"What was he doing?"

"He was half in a big bin they use to store chains and rope and stuff. When I asked him if he'd seen Von, he came out of there so fast, he hit his head. When I asked him what he was looking for, he turned all red and swore at me. Tough talk for a weakling like him. Then Von came in and told him to get lost. I guess he ran to Mama, because by the time Von and I took the first swings, she ran out there and started screaming at us."

"What do you think he was looking for?" Chris asked.

"I have no idea, but maybe you ought to ask him."

"I will."

Trey went into the house and Chris turned back to the ATV. He'd check the VIN with the list Willow had given him, but he was sure the vehicle belonged to the Russell ranch. When he got back to town, he'd see about getting someone up here to haul it in. Maybe they'd get some evidence off it, though he didn't hold out much hope.

He walked back to his cruiser, but stopped at the entrance to look back toward the trailer. The curtains twitched at the far window, and for a fraction of a second, someone looked out at him. Trey had claimed his girlfriend, Courtney Baker, wasn't home, but Chris could have sworn he had just seen her. But the window was empty again, the curtain still. Had Trey deliberately lied to him, or simply been mistaken? Maybe Chris would ask Shane Ellis if his fiancée, Courtney's sister-in-law, had seen Courtney lately.

In the meantime, work was piling up on his desk, and he didn't feel any closer to finding Sam's murderer or helping Willow Russell.

WILLOW LED DARLA and Emmet to the horse barn and showed them how to feed and water the animals. "When you're done with that, you'll need to clean the stalls," she said.

"What are you going to do?" Emmet asked.

"I'm going to place an order for feed, then I'm going to pay bills."

"I could do that," Darla said. "Pay the bills, I mean. I'm good with paperwork."

Willow had no intention of letting Darla rummage through the ranch finances. Even if Emmet eventually ended up owning half the ranch, the financial details of her father's estate were none of Darla's business. "I'll handle the bills," she said. "If you want to do something else to help, you can clean up around the entrance. Von was supposed to rake up the coals and cut the dead trees, but he didn't do it."

"I'm not some ranch hand you can order around," Darla said.

"My father had a saying," Willow said. "You probably heard it when the two of you were married. He said, 'If you don't work, you don't eat.' Until I find someone to take Von's place, all three of us have to work to keep things going. If you can't agree to that, you can leave." She looked Darla in the eye, determined to stare her down.

"Come on, Mom." Emmet picked up a feed bucket. "We can do this."

Willow left them and returned to the house. She'd have to check their work later, to make sure the horses were properly cared for. Meanwhile, she kept her fingers crossed someone would respond to her advertisement for help.

She decided to take care of the bills before she left the house, partly to keep tabs on Darla and Emmet, and partly in case she needed to stop by the bank while she was in town and transfer funds between accounts.

She sat behind the desk, the worn leather chair embracing her, the leather-and-aftershave scent of her father faint in the air, as if his ghost lingered in this place where he had spent so much of his life. She pulled the ledger from the drawer and flipped through it. The pages were labeled for various spending categories—feed, veterinary care, supplies, repairs and so on. The last section was headed "Labor," with line after line indicating wages paid to various ranch workers, including Von King.

She studied the entries more closely. It appeared her father had paid Von a set amount per week, and withheld taxes, so that the check was the same amount each week. She simply had to prorate the amount for the partial week Von had worked.

She took out the checkbook for the ranch account, and flipped the ledger to a new page to record the payment, but stopped when she saw a note in her father's neat handwriting at the top of the page. The note was dated for the Saturday before her father's death on Tuesday, "Terminated," and below that, an entry for a payment, with the notation "Final Paycheck."

Chapter Thirteen

Monday morning found Chris poring over a spreadsheet recording water draws on the local irrigation district. The district manager sent him the reports each week and Chris always read them, looking for anything unusual that might indicate theft or misuse. But he never found anything, and reading the reports reminded him a little too much of his old law firm days.

Besides, he was too distracted lately by thoughts of Willow Russell. More than once over Sunday, his day off, he had started to call and check on her, but he didn't want to come across as pushy. She had promised to let him know if she needed his help, and while he knew she didn't especially like Darla and Emmet, their alibis for the time of Sam Russell's death had checked out, and he didn't think they would do more than annoy Willow. And their presence at the ranch might keep the real killer from trying to get close to her right now.

"Hey, Chris, do you have a minute?"

He pushed his laptop to one side and looked up

at Deputy Jamie Douglas. “Sure. What can I do for you?”

She pulled up a chair and sat. “This morning I finished up questioning the neighbors who live near Carstairs Park,” she said. “Only one of them had anything interesting to say.”

“Did they see someone near the park the morning Sam Russell was killed?” Chris asked.

“He said he saw Adam Treadwell. He was sure it was Treadwell, because they sometimes play golf in the same foursome. But he was surprised to see him out so early.”

“What time was this?”

“Seven thirty. Mr. Geary—Mick Geary—had knee replacement surgery scheduled for that morning and he was getting ready to leave for the hospital.”

“What was Treadwell doing?”

“Mr. Geary said he was running, like he was running from something. He wasn’t dressed for jogging, and he wasn’t on the bike path. He was cutting across the grass from the pond, running hard. Geary wondered what was up, but he had to leave to get to the hospital and what with his surgery and all, he forgot about the incident until I questioned him.”

“Did you ask Treadwell about it?” Chris asked.

“I stopped by his house but his wife said he wasn’t at home. I asked her to have him call me, but so far he hasn’t.”

“Great.” She stood as Shane walked past.

“Hey, Shane.” Chris flagged him down.

Shane stopped beside Chris’s desk. “What’s up?”

"Has Lauren talked to Courtney lately?" Chris asked. "In the last day or two?"

"I don't know," Shane said. "Why?"

"Could you ask her?"

Shane pulled out his phone and typed out a text. "What's going on?" he asked Chris after he had sent the text.

"It may be nothing," Chris said. "But when I was out at their trailer Saturday, Allerton told me I couldn't talk to Courtney because she wasn't there. But as I was leaving, I could have sworn I saw her looking out the window at me."

"Was her car there?" Shane asked. "A white Toyota 4Runner."

"I didn't see it, but it could have been parked around back. Maybe Allerton didn't know she'd returned home."

Shane's phone buzzed and he answered it. "Hey... No, nothing's wrong. Just following up on Allerton's movements." He listened for a moment. "Okay. No big deal. Thanks."

He ended the call and looked at Chris and Jamie. "Lauren said it's been a few days since she's seen Courtney. Lauren has been busy at the clinic where she works. Why did you want to talk to Courtney?"

"I asked Allerton if Von King might have been the one to fire those shots at him," Chris said. "Allerton insisted the shots were from hunters and he said Courtney shouldn't have said anything to us. Then I asked about the snake someone put in his truck and he acted as if he had no idea what I was talking about. I wanted to get Courtney's side of the story, and that's when he told me she wasn't there."

"Trey Allerton always struck me as shifty," Jamie said. "Though his biggest mistake so far seems to be associating with questionable characters—first Tom Chico, and now Von King."

"Courtney seems happy with him," Shane said. "And it takes all kinds."

"He strikes me as someone who's full of a lot of talk and little action," Chris said. "He talks about how much work needs to be done on his so-called 'ranch,' but I never see him doing anything."

"I think Trey thinks of himself as the idea man," Shane said. "While other people do the heavy lifting. We think he's gotten a lot of money from Courtney, but we can't see that he's spent much on that ranch." He slid his phone back into his pocket. "Lauren and I will stop by soon to check on Courtney."

"See what you can find out about the feud between Allerton and Von." Chris stood. "Maybe Courtney knows something Allerton hasn't told us."

"I will," Shane said. "Where are you off to?"

"I'm going to track down Adam Treadwell. I want to find out what he was doing in Carstairs Park Tuesday morning—and why he neglected to tell us he was there."

CHRIS TRACKED DOWN Adam Treadwell at the driving range on Idlewilde Estates's golf course. Treadwell looked up at Chris's approach. "Hello, Deputy." Treadwell smiled, a toothy grin that showed no hint of unease. "Did you find out who dumped that ATV in our pond?"

Chris refrained from pointing out that the pond actually belonged to the irrigation district. "Not yet," he said. "But I did want to ask you some more questions about that morning."

"Sure." He straightened and slotted his driver into his golf bag. "Why don't we sit over here in the shade?" He led the way to a picnic table beneath a wooden shelter. He slid onto the bench and Chris settled opposite him.

"Tell me again where you were Tuesday morning," Chris said.

"I was at home."

"Alone?"

"Yes. My wife was in Denver, visiting a friend. Why?" Treadwell laughed. "You don't think I dumped that ATV in the pond, do you?"

"We have a positive ID from a credible witness who saw you in the park Tuesday morning, around seven thirty," Chris said.

Treadwell's face paled beneath his tan, though his smile remained rigid. "Who told you that?"

"Our witness was positive about the identification. Why don't you tell me what you were doing in the park then."

Treadwell looked away, fingers drumming the picnic table. Then he relaxed. "I remember now. My wife has been after me to get more exercise, so I made a point of getting up early that morning and going for a walk. Unfortunately, the habit didn't stick." He shook his head. "I guess I got my days mixed up when you asked about it earlier."

"Did you see anyone else while you were out?" Chris asked.

"I sure didn't." Another grin. "Though I guess someone saw me."

"Our witness says you were running."

Treadwell's laugh sounded forced. "Right. At one point I thought maybe I should try jogging. I didn't get very far." He looked out over the driving range. "I guess golf is more my kind of exercise."

"The witness said you looked like you were fleeing—running away from something."

All pretense of an easy manner vanished. "Are you accusing me of something? It's not against the law to be in the park at seven thirty in the morning."

"You and Sam Russell exchanged some pretty harsh words during your argument about the home-owners' pollution of the irrigation ditch," Chris said.

"Alleged pollution," Treadwell said. "The water was never tested."

"Still, you both lost your tempers."

"We did." Treadwell bowed his head, silent for a long moment. Chris watched him, waiting. When Treadwell looked up again, his gaze was unflinching. "Look, I didn't like Sam," he said. "I thought he was one of those old-timers who is determined to oppose anything new. We were never going to see eye to eye about the water issue. But I didn't kill him. I wouldn't. I'm not a violent person."

Chris thought anyone might be pushed to violence, but Adam Treadwell had no criminal record of any kind. The man had never even had a traffic ticket. And the timing of the sighting troubled Chris. If Sam was killed at the earliest edge of the medical examiner's estimated time of death, a man racing the ATV alongside the Daimler Ditch might have made it to the park by seven thirty, but it would be pushing it. He stood. "We're still checking the ATV for prints and other evidence," he said. "I'll be in touch if we find anything."

Treadwell nodded. He looked relieved at this news. "I hope you find whoever did it," he said. "I never liked Sam, but I wouldn't wish murder on anyone."

WILLOW NEVER MADE it back to town that weekend. Shortly after her discovery that her father had fired Von King, the farrier arrived and she had to accompany him as he cared for the feet and teeth of all the horses. The next day, haying began. It was Monday afternoon before she could get away, and instead of going to Eagle Mountain, she set out for the cabin where Von King had lived on the ranch.

She drove her father's truck. Her own compact car practically rattled her teeth loose on the rough gravel roads that cut through the ranch. Besides, she liked driving the big, powerful vehicle. She liked sitting up high above the road, and taking in the view through the broad expanse of windshield. Here, as in her father's office, his scent lingered—saddle soap and Old Spice and the cigars her mother had long ago forbidden him to smoke in the house.

Von, like a series of farmhands before him, had lived in a log cabin built in the early 1900s in a grove of cottonwoods by the side of the Daimler Ditch. The building was a squat rectangle, maybe thirty-two feet by sixteen feet, a series of three square rooms with a tiny bathroom cobbled onto the far end sometime in the 1950s. A small stable out back had room for a horse or two, though just as often these days one of the ranch ATVs parked in the stall. A personal horse wasn't an expense every hand could afford. When they needed to ride, they borrowed a mount from the ranch string.

Willow parked in the gravel in the shade of one of the leafy cottonwoods and studied the house. It looked empty. Certainly there was no sign of Von's truck around, and Willow had not seen or heard from him all weekend. She opened the door of the truck and slid out. Though she had driven past this place hundreds of times over the years, she had never been inside. She had never had a reason to come here. The men who worked for her father were usually solitary, older than her, without wives she might have befriended or children she could have played with. Some of the hands had been friendly to her, but most had ignored her.

Von had not ignored her. He seemed to have taken a dislike to her the moment she moved back to the ranch. She had thought it was because she was a woman, but she wondered now if he had another reason. Had he seen her as intruding on or influencing his relationship with her father? Hers were another pair of eyes to watch him and maybe see when he was up to no good.

She squared her shoulders and walked up onto the porch. The door was unlocked and she eased it open. She didn't know what she had expected to find, but the disorder inside was worse than she had feared. It took a moment for her to register that the jumble of items in the room wasn't the result of slovenly habits, but deliberate destruction. She picked her way through broken chairs, smashed dishes and scattered trash. Von must have thrown a regular temper tantrum. She took out her phone and snapped a few photos, then moved to the next room, determined to complete the inspection.

This was the bedroom, with an unmade bed and a dresser with every drawer pulled out onto the floor. She opened the closet and studied the jumble of items there—a boot with a broken heel, its mate lying on its side at the back of the closet. A power drill. A dented thermos. With a start, she realized these things had belonged to her father. She had given him the boots several Christmases ago, and when she turned over the thermos, her father's initials were engraved on the side.

She straightened, still staring at the sad collection. Had her father given Von these things? She shook her head. Her father wasn't one to pass along hand-me-downs.

Had Von stolen the items? That seemed a more

likely explanation, and it could have been the reason Sam had fired Von.

But why had Von decided to keep working after her father died? With his perpetual scowl, it wasn't as if he ever appeared to enjoy the work.

But maybe jobs were hard to find for ex-cons and Von had wanted desperately to hang on to this one.

Desperately enough to kill?

Chapter Fourteen

Monday afternoon, Chris returned to the Russell ranch. He knocked on the door of the ranch house, but no one answered. He walked to the edge of the porch and surveyed the yard. There was no sign of movement anywhere. He walked over to the machine shed, which was empty.

When he started toward his cruiser again, he thought he heard music. He followed the sound to the horse barn, where he found Emmet cleaning a stall. The younger man wore cargo shorts, a T-shirt with a cartoon of an alien, and tennis shoes, unlikely attire for a ranch hand.

Emmet stopped his work and leaned on the shovel. “Need something, Deputy?”

“I’m looking for Willow.”

“She drove off a little while ago.”

“Where’s your mother?” Chris asked.

“I don’t know. I don’t think she’s speaking to me right now, which is fine by me.”

“Why isn’t she speaking to you?”

"I told her I wanted to go back to Albuquerque. But she's determined to stay, so I guess I'm stuck."

"I heard you could inherit half the ranch," Chris said. "Did you know about that before Sam died?"

"I didn't know anything about it until Mom told me while we were driving here, after the old man died."

"Were you surprised?"

"Well, yeah. I mean, I always knew Sam had pots of money, but he didn't like to part with it. He didn't even trust banks, just kept his loot hidden around the ranch."

Chris recalled that Darla had mentioned something like this to Willow. "Do you mean Sam kept a lot of money in his safe?" he asked.

"I heard he stashed it different places. He had so much money he probably didn't even keep track." Emmet shrugged. "Not that I've seen any of it."

"Is that what you were doing in the machine shed the other day?" Chris asked. "Were you looking for hidden cash?"

Emmet flushed. "Maybe. There's no law against looking, is there? And half of it's mine now, anyway."

"Did you see the will?" Chris asked.

"No. All that legal mumbo jumbo wouldn't mean anything to me, anyway."

"Why would Sam leave the money to you?"

"Mom says I'm the son Sam always wanted and never had, but really, I think she talked him into it. It's not like he ever liked me or anything. Or maybe he was upset with Willow and did it to get back at her."

This struck Chris as odd. "Why would he be upset with Willow?" he asked.

Emmet scratched the back of his head. "Well, you know she can be pretty smart-mouthed for a woman. If she doesn't like something, she's not shy about telling you to your face."

"And Sam didn't like that?"

"What man would? I like a woman who's a little easier to get along with. Willow is pretty enough, but when she opens her mouth to lecture you about something, it kind of spoils the effect."

The words grated, but Chris reined in his temper. He had never wanted a woman who wouldn't say what she really thought or felt. Why was that kind of honesty viewed as a negative trait by men like Emmet?

"Are you done asking questions?" Emmet straightened and gripped the shovel again. "Because I've got work to do. Willow will pitch a fit if I don't have this done by the time she gets back. Not that I'm afraid of her or anything. It's just easier to pick up the shovel than to listen to her harp at me."

Chris left him to the work. He was climbing into the cruiser when he spotted a vehicle headed toward him. He recognized the ranch truck, with Willow at the wheel. "I'm glad you're here," she said when he walked out to meet her, and for a moment his heart lifted at the words. Then he realized from her solemn expression that her words had nothing to do with personal pleasure at seeing him.

"What's up?" he asked.

"I found something else you need to see."

She led the way inside and headed for Sam's office, Chris at her heels. They both drew up short when the door opened and Darla emerged. The older woman gasped and put a hand to her chest. "My goodness! You startled me," she said.

"What were you doing in Dad's office?" Willow asked.

"I was looking for a stamp."

"That area is private. You need to stay out of it." Willow took a step forward and Darla scuttled past, but she stopped a few feet away and drew herself up to her full height.

"I'll go anywhere I like in this house," she declared.

Willow glared at her, then moved into the office. Chris followed and shut the door behind them. "I thought you bought a lock for this door," he said.

"I did. I just haven't gotten around to installing it. But I'll make it a priority now." She studied the desk, which was strewn with ledgers and papers. "I'm sure she was snooping around in here, but I left everything in such a mess I can't tell." She moved behind the desk, opened the bottom drawer and took out a ledger. "This is one of the things I wanted to show you." She opened the ledger, flipped through a few pages, then passed it to him. "Read this."

He studied the ledger entries, which appeared to

be a payroll record for Von King. "Check the next page," Willow said.

He turned the page and blinked at the bold writing: "Terminated," followed by "Final Paycheck." "He fired Von."

"That's dated the Saturday before Dad was killed," Willow said.

"You didn't know about this?" Chris asked.

She shook her head. "Dad never said anything. I don't like Von, so I avoided him, and he has days off. I didn't think anything about not seeing him around that Monday. But he was working in the machine shed Tuesday morning, as if nothing had happened."

"Is it possible he had patched things up with your dad? Talked his way back into a job?"

"If he had, Dad would have made a note of it, I'm sure." She took out her phone. "There's something else. This morning, I drove out to the cabin where Von lived." She passed over the phone and Chris looked at the photos of broken furniture and general disarray.

"He trashed the place," Chris said.

"Check the last photo."

He scrolled to the image of a pair of boots, a drill and a thermos. "Those are all things that belonged to my dad," Willow said. "They were all stashed in Von's bedroom closet, like a pile of treasures assembled by a pack rat."

"Maybe Sam gave them to Von."

"I don't think so," she said. "I think Von stole them. He probably took other things, too. I believe that's why Dad fired him. Maybe Dad threatened to turn him over to the sheriff. If he had a prior conviction, wouldn't that make things worse for him?"

He nodded. "Do you know where Von is now?" he asked.

She shook her head and rubbed her hands up and down her folded arms. "But the sooner you find out, the better I'll feel." Her eyes met his. "If he killed my dad for firing him, what will he try to do to me, now that I've done the same?"

CHRIS HADN'T LIKED leaving Willow at the ranch. But she had assured him she would be careful, and she would call 911 right away if she spotted Von King. And she had pointed out that even though Darla and Emmet weren't her favorite people, their presence on the ranch with her offered some protection.

At the sheriff's department, Chris headed straight for Travis's office. "I think we should pick up Von King and bring him in for questioning," he told the sheriff. "Willow found evidence that her father fired Von the Saturday before Sam was killed. Apparently, Von had been stealing from the ranch and Sam found out about it. After Sam died, Von pretended he still had a job and didn't say anything to anyone."

Travis nodded. "All right. Pick him up and bring him in."

"We have to find him first." Chris raked a hand through his hair. "Willow fired him Saturday, before she found out her father had already done so. King cleared out, but not before he trashed the cabin where he'd been living. He didn't leave a way for her to get in touch. Now she's worried that if Von killed her father, he might go after her next."

"Is she alone at the ranch?" Travis asked.

"She has her former stepmother and the stepmother's son there with her, and she intends to hire a new ranch hand to replace Von." He hesitated. "And I intend to spend as much of my off-duty hours there as she'll let me." He hadn't really discussed this with Willow, but he'd made up his mind on the drive back to town that he needed to stick closer to her.

Travis nodded. "We'll put out an APB for Von. We can arrest him on theft charges and hold him on that while we question him."

Some of the tension eased from Chris's shoulders. "Thanks."

"We've got the ATV and trailer from the Russell ranch in our impound lot," Travis said. "Do you think Von was behind that also?"

"I think so. I think leaving it in Trey Allerton's way is part of his feud with Allerton—but we don't have any proof."

"It's one more thing to question him about. What's on your schedule for this afternoon?"

"Perry Webber left me a voice mail a little while ago. He wants me to check out what looks like an illegal diversion ditch in Idlewilde Estates."

Travis nodded. "How did it go with Adam Treadwell earlier?" he asked. "Jamie said you went to question him about his activities Tuesday morning."

Chris shook his head. "He gave me a story about

going for a walk. Then he said he was jogging. Then he got defensive."

"The timing isn't quite right for him as the murderer," Travis said.

"Unless we're off on the time of death for some reason," Chris said. "I think he could have done it if he had really raced the ATV down that path alongside the ditch. He ditches the ATV in the park, then runs home."

"We'll keep digging," Travis said. "When you get a chance, ask Willow to compile a list of things Von stole from her father or the ranch."

"Yes, sir."

On the drive to Idlewilde Estates, Chris's phone rang. The dashboard screen showed the call was from his father. He hesitated before answering, but if Dad suspected Chris was avoiding him, it would only increase the tension between them. "Hello," he answered.

"Hello, Chris," Ted said. "Your mother and I want you to come to dinner Wednesday evening."

"I'm working a case right now," Chris said. "I don't know if I can get away."

"You can find time for dinner. There's someone I want you to meet."

Chris's gut tightened. Those words from his father had never turned out well, from the colleague's daughter he had wanted Chris to date to another friend's business opportunity that had turned out to be a scam. "Who is it?" he asked.

"David Vandermeyer is with the state attorney

general's office. They're looking for someone with a background in Colorado water law. I told him you'd be perfect for the position. He's very interested in meeting you."

"Dad, I already have a job."

"Vandermeyer was impressed with your on-the-ground experience, but it's time to move on from that. This is a terrific opportunity that could lead to even bigger things in the future. And I can guarantee it pays a lot more than you'll ever make working for the county."

As usual, his father was charging ahead with what he wanted for Chris, with no regard for what Chris wanted for himself. "I'm not interested," he said.

"How do you know if you don't even talk to this man?" Ted asked. "This isn't doing grunt work in some big firm, the way you were before. At least hear what he was to say."

It was impossible to fight his dad when he was being so reasonable. "I'll see if I can get the time off," Chris said.

"Do you need me to speak to the sheriff? I will."

"No. Don't do that." He wasn't a kid who needed an excused absence from class. "I'll take care of it."

"Good. Come at six thirty. We'll eat at seven."

Ted ended the call and Chris braked hard to allow a doe and twin fawns to cross the highway in front of him. As he watched the deer, he took several deep breaths, willing himself to calm down. His father loved him and wanted what was best for him, even if he never listened to what Chris thought was best for himself.

Fine. He could go to dinner and listen to the state lawyer, politely thank him for the opportunity and move on. Vandermeyer likely wouldn't understand. Maybe most people wouldn't. But this—spending his days behind the wheel of his cruiser, talking to people from all walks of life, doing everything from mediating a dispute between ranchers to writing a speeding ticket to investigating a murder—this was what made him want to get out of bed in the morning and mostly made him satisfied at the end of the day. All the money and prestige of a state job was never going to feel like that.

He found the address the ditch rider had given him, a sprawling gray stone house encircled by a black wrought-iron fence. Chris was halfway down the side of the fence when a muscular Doberman rushed at him, barking furiously.

A slender man who appeared to be in his seventies followed the dog to the fence. "Can I help you, Deputy?" he shouted over the dog's barking.

Chris eyed the dog and moved closer. "Could you put the dog inside so we can talk?"

The man nodded and dragged the still barking and lunging dog away. He returned a few minutes later. "Come around to the gate," he said, and gestured toward the front of the house.

At the gate, Chris showed his identification. The man introduced himself as Gerald Pierce. "We've had a report of an illegal ditch diverting water from the irrigation canal," Chris said.

Pierce frowned. "I'm not sure I understand," he said.

"I need to inspect the irrigation canal where it runs behind your property," Chris said.

Pierce's frown deepened, until his bushy eyebrows almost met in the middle. "There's no damage to the canal," he said.

"I need to inspect it," Chris said, keeping his voice and his expression firm.

Reluctantly, Pierce led him toward the back of the property. Chris had to admit what he found impressed him. He had expected a crude trench cutting into the Daimler Ditch to divert a stream of water. Instead, Pierce—or someone he had hired—had built a concrete-lined canal with a series of miniature locks to bring water up from the ditch to an area of the backyard enclosed by chain-link fencing. The fencing was lined with green shade cloth. Chris studied the structure. "This all must have taken you some time to build," he said.

Pierce straightened. "I was an engineer before I retired. I enjoy projects like this."

Chris nodded toward the enclosure. "What are you growing?" he asked, though he already had a good idea.

"It's all perfectly legal," Pierce said.

Chris walked over to the fence, which was only about five feet high, so he could clearly see inside. The roughly ten-square-feet space was crowded with a small forest of marijuana plants. Chris stopped counting when he reached twenty.

"It's not illegal to grow cannabis for personal use in this state," Pierce said.

"No, sir, but there is a limit of six plants per person or twelve per household."

"My son and his wife live with us, and we have medical licenses, which allow us to grow more. You'll see that the area is enclosed, not visible to neighbors or the street, and there's a lock on the gate."

Chris nodded. He'd taken required courses on the state's drug laws, and this was in line with what he remembered. He looked Pierce in the eye. "What do you need so much pot for?" he asked.

"My wife and I use it for medical purposes."

"There's enough here you could sell it."

"I don't. I might gift it to a friend occasionally, but we never sell it. That would be against the law."

Pierce might be worth taking a closer look at, but his pot crop wasn't why Chris was here, at least not directly. "You're going to have to find some other way to water your grow," he said. "The plants might not be illegal, but taking water from the irrigation ditch is." He delivered his routine lesson on why Pierce did not have rights to the water that ran by his house.

Pierce listened, growing more glum by the minute. "Is it possible for me to purchase a share of the water rights?" he asked.

"I'm afraid not," Chris said. "Most of them are

passed down through families. Occasionally a share comes up for sale, but not often."

Pierce looked to his fancy system of locks and sighed. "I was really pleased with how the watering system turned out."

"You'll have to dismantle it," Chris said. "Right away. I'll come back tomorrow to check and if it's still operational, you can be fined seven hundred and fifty dollars a day."

Pierce nodded. "I understand."

Chris gave Pierce his card and let himself out the front gate. He was walking to his cruiser when his phone rang.

"Are you still out at Idlewilde?" Adelaide asked.

"Yes."

"We just got another Peeping Tom complaint from a woman there. Audrey Clements." Adelaide rattled off an address. "She says it happened earlier this morning and her husband finally convinced her she should call. You need to go by and take her statement."

Chapter Fifteen

The Clements residence was only a couple of streets over from the Pierces. Audrey Clements and her husband, Bruce, met Chris at the door of the Southwest-style adobe home. They were a trim, slight couple with matching short-cropped gray hair and the deep tans of people who had spent a lifetime outdoors. "I feel bad getting you all the way out here for what is probably nothing," Audrey said as she led the way into the living room.

"It's not nothing." Bruce put a hand on his wife's shoulder and addressed Chris. "Audrey is not the type of person who imagines things. She told me she saw a man looking in our bedroom window while she was undressing this morning and I believe her."

"Bruce ran outside but he didn't see anyone," Audrey said. "And it was very early. Still dark out. So maybe it was just a deer or some other animal."

"Some of Audrey's friends have been talking about a Peeping Tom in the neighborhood," Bruce said.

"Sally Coe said she heard a rumor that there was

a man who was looking in windows," Audrey said. "But I just couldn't believe..." She spread her hands. "I'm sixty years old. What kind of thrill is someone getting looking at me?"

"Let's sit down and you can tell me what you saw." Chris motioned toward the sofa.

They sat, the Clementses side by side, his arm around her shoulder. "I had just pulled my nightshirt off, getting ready to take a shower," Audrey said. "I glanced toward the window. The weather is so nice, we've been sleeping with the window open. And there was, well, a shadow. A man-shaped shadow. I gasped and covered myself with the nightshirt and whoever it was ran away."

"Did you see his face?" Chris asked.

She shook her head. "He really did look like a shadow. I think he must have been wearing all black."

"How tall was he?"

She looked at her husband. "Not tall. Maybe Bruce's height."

"I'm five-eight," Bruce said.

"Was he fat or thin?" Chris asked.

"Just...average." She shrugged. "I'm sorry, but I really only caught a glimpse of him."

"Which direction did he head when he ran away?"

"West. Toward the backyard." She looked puzzled. "I would have thought he would head for the street."

"Have you had any other reports like this?" Bruce asked.

"We've had at least one other," Chris said. He stood. "If you think of anything else, call me." He handed Audrey his card. "And if the man comes back, call 911."

"Thank you." She shook her head. "I felt silly even calling you, but it is upsetting."

"I'm glad you called. The more information we have, the more likely we are to catch this person."

He returned to his cruiser, but didn't start it right away. He studied the Clements house, then pulled up a map of Idlewilde Estates on the computer unit in his cruiser. The Clementses lived on Lodgepole Lane. The woman who had made the previous complaint lived on Ash Drive. The park was flanked by Ash Drive and Cedar Court. Aspen Lane ran between Ash and Cedar.

And Adam Treadwell lived on Aspen. Adam Treadwell, who had been seen running from the park—running from the direction of Cedar—last Tuesday morning. The same morning the woman had called in a complaint about a Peeping Tom.

Chris started the cruiser. Time to have another conversation with Adam Treadwell.

WILLOW STOOD BACK, arms crossed as the locksmith finished installing the new lock on the office door. He inserted the key and turned it, tried the door, then opened it again and removed the key. "That should do you," he said, and handed Willow the key.

"Thank you." Willow pocketed the key and accepted his bill. She paid him and he left.

Darla entered as the locksmith left. "Who was that?" Darla asked. "What was he doing here?"

"That was a locksmith. I had him install locks on my bedroom door and on the door of my dad's office."

"Why did you do that?" Darla asked.

"To keep out people who don't have any business in those rooms."

Darla sniffed. "I hope you're not planning on continuing to live here after Sam's will is probated," she said.

"Why not?" Willow asked.

"Because half the ranch will belong to Emmet and he intends to sell. You'll have to sell, too. It's not as if you ever wanted to run the ranch, anyway. Your father knew that. It's one of the reasons he left half the property to Emmet."

"The ranch is in a conservation easement," Willow said.

Darla waved away this objection. "You can still sell it. Whoever buys it simply has to agree to keep it as a ranch. This place is a moneymaker, so it won't be hard to find a buyer."

"First, you have to prove your will is valid," Willow said.

"Are you accusing me of lying?" Darla asked.

"I guess the court will decide that."

"Your father would be very disappointed by your attitude," Darla said. "Then again, you often disappointed him. You could have been such a help to him. Instead, you insisted on moving away, only running home when you needed something from him." She sighed and shook her head. "Such a shame."

She left the room, leaving Willow to stare after her, angry tears stinging her eyes. Part of her realized Darla had been trying to make her angry. She told herself she shouldn't take the bait. But there was enough truth behind the words that they provoked real pain. Willow had disappointed her father—not because she'd wanted to hurt him, but because she could never be the person he'd wanted. The knowledge that he had never understood or accepted that had hurt, and now that he was gone, they would never have a chance to heal that old wound.

ADAM TREADWELL CLEARLY wasn't pleased to see Chris. "What do you want, Deputy?" Treadwell demanded when he answered Chris's knock on his door.

"I need to come in and ask you some more questions," Chris said.

"I'm busy right now."

Treadwell started to close the door, but Chris blocked the move. "If you don't want to talk to me now, we can go down to the station to do it."

Treadwell hesitated, then stepped back. "You can come in," he said. "But I can't give you much time."

They moved into the living room—aspen paneling, a large entertainment center, a bookcase with golf tournament trophies. "Is your wife home?" Chris asked.

"She's upstairs. There's no need to disturb her. What is this about?"

"We've had another report of a Peeping Tom in the neighborhood," Chris said.

Treadwell stiffened. "What does that have to do with me?"

"I thought as homeowners' association president, you'd want to know."

"There's nothing I can do about it," Treadwell said. "It's probably some kid playing a prank and the women are overreacting."

"I don't think this is a kid."

"It doesn't matter to me what you think. I really need to go. I'm going to be late for my appointment." He started to move toward the door again.

"What were you really doing in the park Tuesday morning?" Chris asked.

The question froze Treadwell in midstride. He turned to face Chris again. "I already told you—I was taking a walk."

"A walk past the Brecks' house on Ash Drive?"

Treadwell's face blanched. "I don't know what you're talking about."

"What about the Clementses' house on Lodgepole Lane? The big adobe? Did you walk by there this morning? Did you stop and look in the window?"

"I don't like what you're implying," Treadwell said. "You need to leave now."

"Adam? Is something wrong?" A slight, blonde woman appeared in the doorway, concern edging her voice.

"It's nothing, Dot. Go back upstairs."

She turned to Chris. "What is it, Deputy?" Her face was pale, but her gaze was steady.

"It's nothing," Treadwell said again, more forcefully.

"Are you Mrs. Treadwell?" Chris asked.

"Yes."

"Were you aware there have been reports of a Peeping Tom in the area?" Chris asked.

She turned to her husband, expression stricken. "Adam, you promised!" she said. "You said it wouldn't happen again."

"Dot, I—" He reached for his wife, but she turned away.

"Mrs. Treadwell, has something like this happened before?" Chris asked.

She nodded. "In Ohio, where we used to live. The police promised not to press charges if Adam would go to counseling. And he did. I thought he had put that all behind him."

"I didn't do anything wrong!" Treadwell protested. "I was just out for a walk. I'm not responsible if people don't keep their shades drawn."

"Mr. Treadwell, I'm going to have to take you in for further questioning," Chris said.

"I'll contact our attorney," Dot said, and left the room without looking at her husband.

"Did you have to do that?" Adam asked, looking after her.

"A better question might be, did you have to?" Chris asked.

"I know your father," Treadwell said.

"A lot of people do."

"What would he think of you, harassing a respectable citizen?"

"I don't think peeping in windows is very respectable."

Treadwell swore at him. Chris moved away to call for backup, and an officer to take a statement from Mrs. Treadwell. They had one less suspect now for Sam Russell's murder, but Chris couldn't say he felt good about it.

"THAT DEPUTY IS BACK." Darla peered out the front window Tuesday afternoon, frowning. "Why does he keep hanging around here?"

"He's trying to find my father's murderer." Willow smoothed her hair and tried to ignore the flutter in her stomach at the thought of seeing Chris again.

"He hasn't found anything yet," Darla said. "And it's annoying having him around all the time."

"Then leave." She gave Darla a cool look.

"I need to get back to Albuquerque," Emmet said. "I'm running out of clothes."

"Hush," Darla said. "You can buy clothes in town."

Emmet rolled his eyes. "As if Eagle Mountain has anything resembling fashion."

There was a knock on the door and Willow hurried to answer it. "Hello, Deputy." She smiled at Chris. "What brings you here?"

"I wish I could say it's because I wanted to see

you—which is true—but I'm actually here on official business."

"Oh." Her smile faded and she stepped back. "Have you arrested someone?" she asked. "Did you find Von?"

"Not yet." He glanced toward the living room, where Darla and Emmet watched from the sofa. "Maybe we should talk in Sam's office."

"Don't keep secrets, Deputy," Darla said.

"Maybe you two should go into town and buy those clothes," Willow said. She led the way to her father's office and shut the door behind them.

"How's the search for help going?" Chris asked.

"I found someone," she said. "Or rather, a neighboring rancher, Darrell Williams, is loaning me one of his cowboys, for as long as I need him."

"That was good of him."

"Yes." She sank into the desk chair. "And it was a good reminder for me that my dad had more friends than he did enemies."

"I spoke to Bud Carstairs. He lives in Junction now, but he told me he didn't have any hard feelings about your dad, and I believe him."

She nodded. "Bud was always a good man. He was already having a hard time keeping up with the ranch work when his wife got sick. Dad hated that he sold the place to developers, but the sale gave Bud the money he needed to look after his wife before she died." She met his gaze. "Enough small talk. Why are you here?"

He unzipped his leather satchel and passed over a

folded paper. "That's a warrant authorizing the sheriff's department to search all your father's papers and anything else in his office. We were waiting for someone from the Colorado Bureau of Investigation to help us with that, but they've been dragging their feet about sending someone, so the sheriff assigned me to do it."

"Oh." She unfolded the paper and stared at it, but the words there didn't really register. She wasn't surprised by the request, only by the enormity of the task. "There are reams of documents in here," she said. "It will take forever for you to go through them all."

"I'm hoping you'll volunteer to help me," he said. "You know what's here better than anyone, and you've already unearthed every break we've had so far. You found out about the feud your dad was having with Adam Treadwell, and that he had fired Von King."

"I don't know if those are breaks, or if they only muddy the waters," she said.

"Will you help?" he asked.

"Of course." She looked around. "Where do you want to start?"

"Do you have a copy of your dad's will?" he asked. "You've told me about it, but I'd like to see it."

"You could have asked your dad to show it to you."

"It's easier this way."

"All right." She opened the top left drawer and took out a legal-size envelope and passed it to him.

"This is a copy of the will your father drew up for my father," she said. "I don't have a copy of the will Darla presented."

"Have you heard any more about that one?" He slid a sheaf of papers out of the envelope and scanned them.

"Ted says he's sent it to an expert who specializes in disputed documents."

"Hmm." Chris flipped through the pages of the will, briefly studying each one. After a few moments, he set the will aside. "I can't see how anyone but you benefits from this will," he said.

"Dad wasn't necessarily killed because of money," she said. "Maybe someone was angry with him. Von was angry because Dad fired him. Dad and Adam Treadwell argued about the irrigation ditch behind Idlewilde Estates."

"We don't think Treadwell killed your father," Chris said.

"Why not? Or are you allowed to say?"

"The story will probably be in the next issue of the paper. At the time your father was killed, Treadwell was skulking through the streets near his house, spying on women who were getting dressed."

She stared, mouth open. "He's a Peeping Tom?"

Chris nodded. "He confessed. He's been in trouble for this before, where he used to live. So that's one less suspect on our list."

"What about Von?" she asked.

"We've alerted every law enforcement office in

the state and we're talking to everyone who had contact with him here, but no word yet."

"Who else is on your suspect list?" she asked.

"It's a long list," he said. "Other than Treadwell, we haven't ruled out anyone yet."

His words sent a shiver of fear through her. "Am I still a suspect?"

"You were closest to your father and you benefit from his will, so you're still on the list," he said. "But there are a lot of people ahead of you."

It wasn't exactly a declaration of his belief in her innocence, but for now it would have to do. She regarded the paper-strewn desk. "Where should we start?"

"Bank statements and the ledger," he said. "Let's see if Sam made any unusual payments in the weeks prior to his death."

"Do you think he was being blackmailed?"

"I'm not assuming anything," Chris said. "I'm just looking for anything that stands out as unusual."

For the next couple of hours, he sat on one side of the desk, she on the other, passing papers back and forth and discussing what they read. "I don't see anything unusual, financially." She sat back and stretched, arching her back to work out a cramp. "Just the usual receipts and payments."

Chris laid aside the ledger he'd been paging through. "Emmet said something when I was here yesterday. He said your dad didn't like banks and he kept most of his money hidden around the ranch."

She laughed. "Leave it to Emmet to latch onto that

old rumor. But as you can see from all these bank statements, Dad had several accounts."

"Emmet was nosing around in the machine shed. He admitted he was looking for hidden cash."

"Do you think that's significant?" she asked.

He shrugged. "It might be a motive for someone to kill Sam—they heard he had a lot of money hidden and they decided to steal it."

"How horrible if that was what happened," she said. "It's terrible enough that he was murdered, but to have died because of a lie..." She stared past him, blinking back tears, weariness settling like a heavy cloak around her shoulders.

Chris's chair squeaked as he stood. "I could use some fresh air," he said. "How about you?"

She nodded, and stood and followed him out of the office, taking care to lock the door behind her. The hallway and living room was empty, though they could hear Darla's muffled voice somewhere in the back of the house. "Let's slip out before she sees us," Willow said.

"Do you want to talk a walk?" Chris asked.

"I've got a better idea," she said. "Do you ride?"

"I'm no expert, but I can stay in the saddle."

"Then let's go for a ride. It will give you a chance to see more of the ranch." And the opportunity for the two of them to do something together that didn't involve hunting a killer.

Chapter Sixteen

Chris managed to saddle and mount the horse Willow chose for him—a bay gelding named Paco—without embarrassing himself. Most of his previous experience with horses involved a few weeks at summer camp as a preteen. Willow, on a pinto named Pete, looked at home in the saddle. "I guess you grew up with horses," Chris said as she led the way up a hill behind the horse barns.

"Yes. Riding was definitely one of the things I missed when I moved away." They crested the hill and turned onto a well-worn path that cut across a stubbled field. "I had a crew in to cut hay here over the weekend," she said.

"So you're doing okay, running the ranch by yourself," he said.

"I wouldn't have remembered the hay if Von hadn't said something about it, but his comment is what prodded me to look at Dad's records. I'm getting a feel for what needs to be done."

"Are you still planning to hire someone to manage the ranch for you?"

"If Emmet inherits half, he wants to sell," she said. "I don't have the money to buy him out, so I'd have to sell, too. Which is probably for the best. As hard as my father tried to instill in me a love for the land and the work, it just didn't take. I loved him. I see the beauty of this place, but it's not how I want to spend my life."

"How do you want to spend your life?" It seemed an idle question, a way to keep the conversation going, but as he waited for her answer, he realized how much he cared about what she might say. Was she going to tell him that she longed to be far away from this place and this life—and him?

"I love teaching," she said. "I got into cultural anthropology because I thought I wanted to be a researcher, but I discovered what I really loved was sharing my knowledge with students and interacting with them."

"Could you teach another subject?" he asked. "If you couldn't find a position with a cultural anthropology department?"

"Sure. But I'm really overqualified for most teaching positions. I might look that direction if I keep getting turned down by the universities I've applied to. Maybe junior college, or even high school..." She shrugged. "I'm telling myself I don't have to worry about it until after the will is probated. Ted says with a contested estate, that could take months."

"As if you didn't have enough stress already," Chris said.

"This is how I de-stress," she said, and nudged her horse into a faster walk.

Paco followed Pete across the hayfield, and for the next ten minutes Chris focused on trailing Willow across the field, through a gate and around another rocky hill. He enjoyed the sight of her curvy figure in the saddle, her long braid flowing behind her. He felt free to admire her without being accused of staring.

They drew up short by a low log cabin, half the roof missing. The structure huddled against a rock outcropping, a short distance from a water tank where a windmill creaked in a faint breeze. "We'll water the horses here," Willow said, swinging out of the saddle.

"What is this place?" Chris asked as he led Paco to the tank.

"I think my great-uncle lived here for a while—my grandmother's younger brother, Ralph. After he died, my dad used it during roundups, sometimes. Then the roof caved in and now it's just another old building on the ranch. There are several—mostly built when my great-grandfather was first settling the place, some before that." She turned to study the cabin while the horses drank. "They're too primitive for anyone to live in—uninsulated, some with broken windows or gaps between logs, or even dirt floors. But they're part of the history of this place."

"I see places like this sometimes when I'm hiking in the mountains," Chris said. He moved to stand closer to her, their shoulders almost touching. The breeze blew the tendrils of hair that had escaped from her long braid, and he caught the floral scent of her shampoo, soft and feminine. “Places where people once lived, in such remote locations.”

“It was a very different life,” she said. “My great-grandmother talked about only going to town every six months. After she married my great-grandfather and moved here, she didn’t see her mother for ten years.”

“That would be hard,” Chris said.

“Yes. Then again, when Dad and I couldn’t see eye to eye about something, I would think maybe a few years apart might improve things between us.” She glanced at him. “And you know I don’t mean that, right? Especially now that he’s gone. Now I’d give anything to argue with him again.” She looked away, but not before he saw the glimmer of tears in her eyes.

“I know what you mean,” he said. “Sometimes I feel that way about my dad, too.”

“I keep forgetting that Ted is your father. The two of you don’t seem that much alike.”

“That’s because we’re not.” He turned to watch the horses, who were cropping grass around the water tank. “I went to law school partly because I knew it was what he wanted. But when I discovered how much I hated working in a law office and went into law enforcement instead, he wouldn’t even try to understand. He thinks I’m throwing my life away.”

“My dad had a version of that song, too.” Her hand rested on his back, warm and reassuring. Intimate.

“He’s insisting I come to dinner Wednesday

night," he said. "He's invited someone who works for the Colorado Attorney General's Office. Dad is hoping I'll make a good impression and this guy will hire me. It's as if he hasn't heard me the dozen times I've said I'm not interested."

"My dad used to fix me up with the sons of all his ranching friends," Willow said. "I was supposed to marry one of them, settle down and have a few children, who could then inherit both places and build a ranching empire. He accused me of deliberately being a snob when I couldn't manage to fall in love with any of them."

He turned toward her. "You win. Being fixed up with potential spouses is worse than being forced to interview over dinner for a job you don't want."

She laughed. "They were all perfectly nice young men, but they all saw me the way my dad saw me—a potential rancher's wife. The loyal helpmate with no ambitions of her own. Mind you, the rancher's wives I know aren't like that. But my dad and those young men thought they were. And that wasn't me."

"I get it," he said. "You want someone who sees you as you are and accepts that." He thought of Emmet and his complaint that Willow was too smart-mouthed. "Come to dinner with me Wednesday," he said. "Having you there will make it easier for me to avoid saying something to my dad that I shouldn't."

She laughed. "Now, that's an invitation I can hardly pass up."

He laughed, too. "Okay, not the suavest move on my part, but will you come to dinner, anyway? If you don't think it's too awkward, dining with your father's lawyer."

"I'd love to have dinner with you," she said. "And your father."

"You've made me so happy I could kiss you."

Her eyes met his, dark and mesmerizingly beautiful. "Then why don't you?" she asked.

He wasn't going to pass up an invitation like that, so he pulled her to him and kissed her, gently at first, then, when she curved her fingers around the back of his neck and arched her body to his, with more intensity.

He had been wanting this almost from their first meeting, always holding himself back, unsure of her feelings for him.

But apparently, she had been wanting this, too. She kissed him with the ardor of a lover, her enjoyment of the interlude adding to his own pleasure. He reveled in the feel of her body against his, in the taste of her and the satin texture of her lips.

When at last they parted, a little breathless, she smiled. "That was nice," she said.

It had been much more than nice, but all he said—all he could manage, really—was a dazed smile of his own and "Yeah."

She smoothed her hand down his arm and twined her fingers with his. "We should get back to the house. Darla and Emmet are probably trying to pick the lock on the office door or climb in the window or something."

"Or Emmet will be pulling up floorboards,

searching for Sam's hidden stash of cash." He went along with her teasing tone, though his mind was still partly on all the things he would like to do if only the two of them had the house to themselves.

"I didn't tell you, but I caught him in the barn loft this morning," she said. "He had actually pried up a loose board. I guess he was looking for Dad's hidden money, though I didn't realize it at the time."

Chris glanced over at the dilapidated cabin. "I guess if you want this place torn down, you could hint that the money is here and he'd take it apart for you."

"That's too much work for Emmet. He rarely does anything unless Darla prods him. I wouldn't be surprised to learn she's behind the money hunt, too."

"Does she have a job?" Chris asked.

"When she and Dad met, she was a receptionist for a truck dealership in Junction. I'm not sure what she's done since then, but I think she has plans to live off the proceeds from the sale of this ranch." She pulled herself up into the saddle and turned her horse to face him. "I guess that gives her a motive for killing Dad, but honestly, I can't see it. Darla is whiny and selfish, but she's not…brutal. And what happened to Dad was brutal."

"Yeah." Chris mounted and maneuvered alongside her. So much for thinking this murder wouldn't intrude on their moment of closeness. "I want to find Sam's killer," he said. "Because it's the right thing to do, and because I want you to have that peace."

"I wouldn't have kissed you if I didn't know that,"

she said. Then she turned her horse and rode away, leaving him to try to keep up.

Willow had to suppress the impulse to gallop the horse all the way back to the house. For once she hadn't sabotaged herself with second-guessing and had been honest with a man about what she wanted—and it had felt so good.

That good feeling carried over as they unsaddled, groomed and fed the horses. But some of her exhilaration faded as they approached the house. "Darla's car is gone," she said, and hurried inside.

Chris caught up with her in the hallway. "Is something wrong?" he asked.

She didn't answer right away, having spotted a note tacked to the office door. "We've gone back to Albuquerque for a couple of days to attend to business," the note read in Darla's neat printing. "Back soon."

"You don't look very happy about this," Chris said, after reading the note over her shoulder.

"Oh, I'm thrilled they're gone." She moved past him toward the living room. "I'm just remembering what happened when she and my dad split up."

She stopped in the middle of the living room and looked around for anything out of place.

"What happened then?" Chris prompted.

"I was visiting at the time," she said. "I knew things were tense, but when I came down for breakfast that morning, my dad was in the kitchen by himself. He told me Darla and Emmet had left. I thought it was for the best, but of course I didn't say so. But then I noticed my mother's fruit bowl was gone." She turned to Chris, the pain of that memory still sharp. "It was a hand-painted pottery bowl my mother purchased on their honeymoon in San Francisco. She kept fruit in it, and Darla had always admired it. And then it was gone."

"You think she took it," Chris said.

"I'm sure she took it," Willow said. "Along with a blown-glass bluebird that always sat in the windowsill, and a crystal-and-gold anniversary clock that had belonged to my grandmother. All of my mother's most beautiful things were gone. My dad said it didn't matter, but it mattered to me." The sensation of being back in that moment three years ago, the hurt of having those treasured items—those memories—taken still stung.

Chris squeezed her shoulder. "I'm sorry you had to go through that," he said.

She nodded and pulled herself together to continue taking inventory of the items in the room. "Is anything missing?" Chris asked.

At that moment, she spotted the empty space on the table beside her father's chair. "There was a globe there," she said, pointing. "It was about the size of a cantaloupe and all the countries were cut from semiprecious stones." She cupped her hands, demonstrating. "I gave it to Dad for Father's Day last year. He really liked it."

"I remember seeing it," Chris said. "Do you think Darla took it?"

"Oh, I know she did. It's her way of asserting her claim."

"Will she bring it back?" he asked.

"No, but it doesn't matter." She shrugged. "The globe belonged to my dad, but I didn't associate it with him the way those other items she took represented my mom. It's not as if she took his watch or his rodeo belt buckle. Those are safe because they're locked in my room."

"You could press charges for the theft of the globe," he said. "And anything else you find missing."

"No. I'll wait and see what she has to say about it when she comes back."

"Do you really think they'll be back?"

"As long as she believes she has a chance at half the ranch, she'll be back."

He moved to stand facing her. "I don't think it's safe for you to stay here by yourself," he said.

"Until you find Dad's killer, I'm not crazy about the idea, either," she said. "But I don't have a choice. A ranch isn't something you can walk away from anytime you like."

"I think until we do find your father's murderer, I should stay here with you," he said. He moved closer, focusing her attention on his solid bulk, the reassuring breadth of his shoulders and the weapon at his side. Chris definitely made her feel safe.

"Are we talking in an official capacity?" she asked.

"Unofficial. Though I'll have to let the sheriff

know. But he didn't object when I ran the idea past him."

"You actually talked to him about it?" She was torn between embarrassment and exhilaration.

"I'm determined to keep you safe."

She opened her mouth to tell him she was a strong, intelligent woman who was capable of looking after herself. But Chris had never suggested she wasn't those things. "Thank you," she said. "I would feel better having you here."

"I keep an overnight bag in the car in case of emergency," he said. "Just show me where to stash it."

She moved in. "I think you should put it in my room." Then she kissed him, and his response let her know he thought that was a very good idea indeed.

Chapter Seventeen

Chris followed Willow to her bedroom, moving by instinct, every sense focused on her: on the curve of her bottom in the faded blue jeans, the scent of her hair when he leaned closer, the softness of her hand in his.

She unlocked the door and led the way inside, and he glanced around, registering that the room was that of a teenager who had left home years before with no intention of remaining. There was a white iron double bed with a pale blue duvet, a single straight chair by the door, a student desk and a bulletin board, which was empty but bore the faint outlines of what must have been pictures and invitations and other souvenirs of high school.

Then Willow locked the door and moved into his arms, and their surroundings receded, no longer important. "Are you still on duty?" she asked, one hand resting just below his shoulder-mounted radio.

"Not for the last hour." He unclipped the radio, then unfastened the Sam Browne belt at his waist and laid them on the chair by the door.

"That's a good start." She undid the top button of his uniform shirt and brushed her fingers across the ballistics vest beneath. "So many layers," she said. "Like unwrapping a present."

He remained still as she unfastened each button, one by one, then pushed the shirt off his shoulders. She stood on tiptoe and kissed the top of his shoulder, then traced her tongue along the collarbone, sending shockwaves of sensation through him.

When she tilted her head and smiled up at him, a teasing light in her eyes, he could wait no longer, and ripped open the fastenings at the side of the vest, then tossed it aside.

"Yes, please," she said, and slid her hands up his chest. He pulled her close and kissed her hard, until they were both breathless. Then he walked her backward to the bed and they collapsed together on the soft duvet.

She traced the indentations the vest had made on his skin. "This doesn't look very comfortable," she said.

"You get used to it." He smoothed his hand down her hip. "And speaking of protection...do you have any?"

She laughed. "That was a smooth segue. And yes, I do."

This brought a host of other questions to mind—had she stocked up because of him, or was it her habit to always be prepared? But then she began unbuttoning her blouse and those thoughts fled.

They didn't say much after that, as they finished

undressing and began the tantalizing pleasure of exploring each other's bodies. She communicated all he needed to know with a lifting of one eyebrow, a shift of her hips, a sigh or moan or shake of her head. He liked that she wasn't shy about letting him know what she liked and that she was bold in trying things he might like—which he did.

He reined in his own urgency, and let her set the pace, desire building. When at last he rolled on the condom and entered her, they were both trembling with need, and it took only a few seconds before they found a rhythm that satisfied them both.

She opened her eyes and held his gaze as they moved together, and he lost himself in that gaze, physical and emotional sensations melding. He felt closer to Willow in this moment than he ever had to any woman, vulnerable, but not afraid. He watched her climax overtake her and gave himself over to the pleasure that crashed through him, until at last they lay spent.

She moved to his side, her head nestled on his shoulder. He felt her lips curve against him. "Are you smiling?" he asked.

"I'm smiling," she said. "Aren't you?"

"I am." As long as he was with Willow, he might not stop, no matter what this case threw at them.

WILLOW WOKE WITH the pale light of dawn shining around the edges of the blinds, and the sensation she wasn't alone. She rolled over to look at Chris, who was asleep on his back, the sheet pushed down to his waist, and she allowed herself the luxury of straight-up ogling him. He was a gorgeous man and she was lucky enough to have him in her bed.

Of course, he was lucky, too, and she credited him as being smart enough to know it. Other men—usually ones she turned down when they propositioned her—had accused her of being too picky. But Willow didn't believe in settling. She wanted the best and Chris Delray was the best man she had met in a long time—maybe ever.

He opened his eyes, and the glint of amusement in them told her he had been awake for a while. "Are you just going to stare, or are you going to move a little closer?" he asked.

She moved closer. In fact, she slid on top of him, straddling his hips, his arousal firm against her.

"That's more like it," he said, and slid his hands up to cup her breasts, then stroked his thumbs across her nipples, sending sensation lancing through her. She pressed against him, rocking gently, unable to keep still as his mouth closed over one nipple. She felt the pull all the way to her toes, and closed her eyes to savor the sensation.

Then he flipped her over, rolling her to her side as if they were wrestling. She laughed and smiled up at him as he now loomed over her. "Is that all right?" he asked.

That he had asked made it more than all right. "It's perfect," she said, and wrapped her legs around his hips.

He blew out a breath. "Give me a second," he

said, and leaned over to retrieve a condom from the nightstand.

She didn't think she would ever get tired of watching him—the play of muscle beneath his skin, the dimple that formed at one corner of his mouth when he grinned, the glazed look of his eyes as desire overtook him. He was gorgeous, and even better, he made her feel gorgeous.

They took their time, drawing out the moments, lingering over kisses and caresses. Laughter seasoned the lust, and the joy of being with him made every sensation more intense, until by the time her climax shuddered through her she wanted to shout with happiness—so she did. He followed with a roar of his own, and then they both dissolved in giggles, giddy with their delight in each other.

Afterward, they lay together, talking about getting up, but not actually moving. "What do you have to do today?" she asked, after his fourth declaration that he really should get up.

"Unless I get called away, I thought we should spend the day going over your father's paperwork."

"What a thrill," she said.

"It's boring, but necessary." He rose up on one elbow to look down at her. "Are you up for it?"

She nodded. "I want to find who did this—whether it's Von, or someone else."

"Me, too," he said. He caressed her cheek. "And this evening is dinner with my folks. Are you still up for that?"

"I am." Not that she wouldn't rather stay here

with him—in this bed—all day and all night. But relationships were about more than sex—or at least, for her they were.

He kissed her. "Thanks," he said. "For everything."

"Oh, don't think I'm not going to make you pay." She snuggled closer, enjoying the sensation of skin on skin. "You might be losing a lot of sleep in the nights to come."

"Is that a promise?" He grinned, a wicked look that made her stomach somersault, and then his lips and hands were on her again, and she forgot all about who might be getting the better bargain.

CHRIS HAD TEXTED his mother early in the day to let her know he was bringing a friend to dinner, but her obvious pleasure at seeing Willow that evening made him cringe inwardly. "I'm so pleased to meet you," she said. "You must be very special, for Chris to bring you to meet us."

And what was Chris supposed to say to that? That Willow wasn't special? Or that he'd mainly brought her to serve as a buffer against his father's demands?

Thankfully, Willow responded graciously. She complimented the house and remarked on the weather and steered his mom away from asking anything too personal.

Chris's mom took Willow's hand and pulled her into the family room, where Chris's dad stood with a stocky man with a thick head of white hair. A striking woman with a blond pageboy cut sat on the sofa.

"Chris, come meet David Vandermeyer," his father said. He turned to the white-haired man next to him. "David, this is my son, Chris. Top third of his class at University of Denver's law program."

Chris shook Vandermeyer's hand. "I'm a deputy with the Rayford County Sheriff's Department now," he said, pretending not to notice his father's frown.

"That must be interesting work," Vandermeyer said.

"I think so," Chris said.

"As I was telling you, Chris's specialty is Colorado water law," Ted said. "That's why the sheriff's department hired him and it's given him the kind of real-world experience that will be invaluable when he returns to law."

Time to change the subject, Chris thought. "What brings you to Rayford County?" he asked Vandermeyer.

For the next few minutes, they enjoyed a pleasant discussion about the Vandermeyers' second home in Idlewilde Estates, then Chris's mom summoned them all to dinner. Mrs. Vandermeyer—Marta—was seated next to Chris, while her husband sat across the table beside Willow.

"I wasn't aware you and Chris knew each other, Willow," Ted said after they had all helped themselves to roast pork.

"We met recently," Willow said.

Silence while everyone considered this. Chris had the feeling everyone was avoiding saying anything about Willow's murdered father.

Vandermeyer broke the awkwardness with what to Chris was an even more awkward topic. "Your father tells me you're interested in applying for an opening we have at the Colorado Attorney General's Office," Vandermeyer said. "I'd be happy to arrange an interview."

"Thank you," Chris said. "But Dad must have misunderstood. I'm very happy with the sheriff's department."

"I think you owe it to yourself to consider this new opportunity," Ted said. His tone was light, but the tight lines around his mouth betrayed his agitation. "You should be making better use of your degree and training."

Chris ignored his father. "I hope you find the right person for the job," he said.

"Did I overhear you say you have a home in Idlewilde Estates?" Willow asked.

"Yes," Vandermeyer said. "We purchased it about four months ago."

"We fell in love with the area," Marta said. "It's exactly the kind of neighborhood we were looking for."

"I know the family who used to own that land," Willow said. "I often played there as a child. You have some lovely views from there."

"That was one of the things that sold us on the place," Marta said.

The conversation segued to more mundane topics, and for the rest of the meal no one mentioned Chris's job prospects. After dessert and coffee the

Vandermeyers said their goodbyes. David handed Chris a business card. "In case you change your mind about that interview," he said. "We could use someone like you."

When the Vandermeyers were gone, Ted turned to Chris, his jaw tight, shoulders stiff. "It wouldn't kill you to go to an interview," he said.

"An interview would be a waste of time for both of us," Chris said.

"This kind of opportunity doesn't come along every day," Ted said.

"I'm not looking for another opportunity," Chris said.

"Your education is wasted where you are now," Ted said.

"I don't agree," Chris said, his anger rising.

"I'm very disappointed in your attitude."

"Then you're going to have to learn from your disappointment. I intend to stay in law enforcement."

He was aware of Willow and his mother watching this exchange. Now his mother spoke up. "Maybe you'll be sheriff someday."

This wasn't about being sheriff or having a powerful position or making a great deal of money. But if he tried to point that out to his parents, would they believe him? Could they conceive of a success that had nothing to do with those things? "I'm doing work I find satisfying, that makes a difference, that I think is important," he said. "I'm sorry if that isn't enough for you."

His father's jaw tightened, as if he was clenching

his teeth, but he said nothing. Chris turned to Willow. "I think we'd better go."

She thanked his parents for the meal and they said their goodbyes. They drove back to the ranch in silence, a full moon bathing the passing landscape in a silvery light. When he turned his truck onto the road to the ranch, Willow spoke. "When I told my father I was going away to school to study anthropology, he told me I was wasting my time," she said. "He wasn't a fan of higher education, but he said if I had to go to college, I should study something practical, like business."

"I guess parents have visions of what their children's lives should look like," Chris said. "When reality doesn't match that vision, they fight it."

"Dad never stopped fighting it," she said. "When I came home he offered to teach me to manage the ranch for him. I told him thank you but I wasn't interested. I know that hurt him." She sighed. "And then he was killed and I've had to learn, anyway."

"But it's not something you want to keep doing," he said, a knot in his stomach from the knowledge that went with it—that doing what she wanted, what she was trained for, meant leaving here. People had long-distance relationships all the time, he told himself. But the thought brought little comfort.

"I'll find something that fits," she said. "The way you've found your fit." She reached over and took his hand. They drove the rest of the way home like that, hands clasped, the silence between them warm and comforting, like a blanket wrapped around both of them. *I'm not going to let her get away*, he thought. No matter what happened, he was going to find a way to build on what had started between them.

Back at the ranch, he helped Willow make the rounds to check on the horses, then went around the house, making sure all the doors and windows were secure. "When I was growing up, we never locked the doors," she said. "But I guess even in the country, times change."

"I don't think anyone would try to break in, especially with my cruiser parked out front," he said. "But it's smart to be safe."

She moved into his arms and they began kissing, when hard pounding on the door startled them. "Open up!" a man's voice shouted. "I need help!"

Chapter Eighteen

Chris moved to the door and flipped the switch for the porch light, then checked the security peep and frowned. "It's Trey Allerton," he said.

The door vibrated with the force of Trey's knock. "Open up!" he shouted.

Chris unlocked the door and opened it a few inches. Willow moved in close to look around him. She remembered Trey as handsome and cocky, a man who coasted through life on charm and looks. Tonight, deep shadows beneath his eyes detracted from his looks, and his easygoing charm had vanished, replaced by edgy tension. "Where is Von?" he demanded.

Willow stepped up beside Chris. "Von is gone," she said. "I fired him."

Trey shook his head. "He didn't go far," he said. "He was at my place not half an hour ago. He took another shot at me and this time he almost got me."

"You'd better come in." Chris held the door open wider.

Trey hurried inside, and glanced around. "You're sure Von isn't here?"

"He isn't here." Willow felt sorry for Trey. He looked so shaken.

"Sit down and tell me everything that happened." Chris led Trey into the living room and urged him to sit on the couch. Chris sat next to him and Willow moved into the chair opposite.

"I was in the trailer with Courtney and Ashlyn," Trey said. "We'd just had dinner when we heard a truck pull up in the driveway. I looked out and saw Von's truck. I told Courtney I didn't want to talk to him, that we would just ignore him. Then he laid on the horn. He yelled that he knew I was in there and if I didn't come out, he'd set the place on fire. I was worried he was wild enough to do it, so I went to the door. I had my phone in my hand and told him I was going to call the sheriff if he didn't leave. Von ought to know I don't have cell service out there, but he either forgot or he didn't care. He pulled out a pistol and would have killed me if I hadn't dived back into the house. Then he got back in his truck and peeled out of there. I thought for sure he was headed here."

"What were you going to do if you found him?" Chris asked.

Trey looked away, mute.

"Are you carrying a gun?" Chris asked.

"I've got a right to defend myself," Trey said.

"Von left here four days ago," Chris said. "If you have any idea where he might be living now, you need to tell us."

"The thing you need to know about Von is that he isn't right in the head," Trey said. "I mean, he believes things that aren't true, like conspiracy theories and stuff. And he lies about everything. Not to mention, he's mean as snakes. He told me stuff he learned how to do in prison—ways to kill people and stuff. I thought he was just trying to impress me, but maybe he really wanted to scare me."

"So where do you think he's hiding?" Chris asked. "Did he ever mention any place to you?"

Trey shook his head. "If I knew, I'd tell you. But I'm saying when you do find him, he's going to lie to you. He'll probably tell you I killed Sam Russell." He didn't look at Willow, but kept his eyes fixed on Chris.

"Why would he say that?" Chris asked.

"Because I think he killed Sam and he knows if you catch him, he'll have to go to prison for the rest of his life. So he wants to blame me."

"Did you kill Sam?" Chris asked. "Or did you help Von do it?"

"No! I liked Sam. He was helping me. I wouldn't kill him."

"Why do you think Von killed him?" Chris asked.

"He said Sam had a lot of cash hidden around the place," Trey said. "Like, hundreds of thousands of dollars. Von wanted that money."

"You could probably use that money, too," Chris said.

"Who couldn't? But I told him that idea was bananas. You don't get the kind of wealth Sam had by sticking your money in a hole in the ground."

"Did Von tell you he was going to kill Sam?" Chris asked.

"No. But he was talking about the money and it's the kind of thing I think he would do."

"Why do you think Von shot at you?" Chris asked.

"Because he's psycho. Or maybe because he knew I heard him talking about wanting to get his hands on the money Sam had hidden." His gaze darted around him, wary. "Which means I could be in even more danger if he finds out I spoke to you."

"You need to report this to the sheriff," Chris said.

"You're a sheriff's deputy, and I'm reporting it to you."

"I'll call this in, but you'll need to come into the station and make a formal statement."

"I'm making my statement to you. I just want you to find Von and stop him. And remember, he's dangerous, and he's definitely armed. That's against the law, isn't it? For a convicted felon to have a firearm?"

"If he has one, yes."

"I know he has one. He shot at me." Trey licked his lips. "When you do find him, you need to call in a SWAT team or something. Take him out before he kills you."

"Are you sure you don't know where Von might be?" Willow spoke up for the first time since Trey's arrival. "Maybe he mentioned a friend in the area?"

"I don't know anything, I swear." Trey took another step back. "I better go. I don't like leaving

Courtney alone this long with a maniac like Von running loose." He turned and dashed out the door to his truck, then sped out of the drive.

Chris and Willow watched from the window until the plume of dust marking Trey's route disappeared. "I don't understand him," Willow said. "Whenever he would come here before, to talk to my dad, he always bragged about his time in the army, like he was trying to impress Dad with how tough he was. Now he's practically hysterical about Von."

"Having someone try to kill you would frighten most people," Chris said.

"Yes, but this goes beyond fear. He seemed almost as worried about what Von might say about him as he was about Von shooting him."

"Sometimes the people who talk the most about their bravery are the first to fall apart under pressure," Chris said.

"Maybe you're right." She turned from the window. "What are you going to do?"

"I need to call this in. I could use the radio, but I'd rather use your phone."

"Of course." She moved away and he went into the kitchen and dialed Travis's number.

Travis answered with his usual greeting. "What's happened?"

"I'm at the Russell ranch. Trey Allerton just showed up here practically hysterical. He claims Von King took another shot at him, and this time he almost didn't miss." He related all the details. "Allerton thinks we should bring in a SWAT team and stop Von before he kills one of us."

"Huh," Travis said. "Did Allerton have any idea of where to find Von?"

"He says no. And he refused to come into the station to give us a formal statement."

"Any sign of Von around the ranch?" Travis asked. "Any more trouble there?"

"No. Darla and Emmet went back to Albuquerque, so I'm sticking close to keep an eye on things."

"Uh-huh. Well, you look after Willow." He ended the call before Chris could say anything else. Chris replaced the phone receiver in the cradle. The sheriff was hard to read. He ran a tight department, with a culture of discipline and training. But he was also married to a woman he had once helped to convict—falsely, as it turned out—of murder. So the idea of one of his deputies being involved with someone close to a murder investigation wasn't foreign to him.

Willow entered the kitchen. "What did the sheriff say?" she asked.

"The sheriff is a man of few words," Chris said. "I told him I was staying here to keep an eye on things, and he seemed to agree that was a good idea."

Willow looked amused. "Well, as long as he agrees." She filled a kettle. "I'm going to make a cup of cocoa. Do you want some?"

He moved in behind her and wrapped his arms around her. "That sounds good."

He set out cups while she heated milk and made the cocoa. Then they carried their mugs into the living room and curled up together on the sofa. It was a domestic, homey scene that filled him with contentment, in spite of his lingering concern over Allerton's visit. "I'm still thinking about Trey's visit—and about Von," Willow said, as if channeling his thoughts.

"Me, too," Chris admitted.

She leaned her head back to look up at him. "What was Von in prison for? Can you tell me?"

"Burglary. Theft. Some assaults. He served five years of a seven-year sentence."

"Maybe someone with that kind of history would kill a man to get to a lot of money he thought the man had hidden," she said. "And since Von never found the money, will he come back to try to get it?"

"I thought you said there isn't any money," Chris said.

"There isn't. But apparently Von doesn't believe that. And I can't shake the image of all those things he'd taken from my dad piled up in his closet—little bits of my father's life that Von stole. Maybe that wasn't enough for him. Maybe he wanted it all."

"He might come back," Chris said. "Or he might never have left."

She looked startled. "What do you mean?"

He leaned forward to set his half-empty mug on the coffee table. "I've been thinking about those old cabins you said were on the ranch. How many of them are there?"

"There's the one I showed you," she said. "And two others."

"Are any of them habitable?"

She frowned. "As in 'move in and spend the next few months'—no. But as a temporary hideout—maybe. You saw the one I showed you—it's pretty wrecked and clearly no one was there when we were. The second one is in even worse shape, more of a ruin than a cabin at this point. But the third…the third is fairly intact. But it's really remote. I mean, you couldn't get there in a vehicle. You'd have to ride a horse or walk."

"I think we need to check it out," he said.

"Now?" She looked alarmed.

"Not now. And not alone. We need backup." He stood and went to the phone. This time it took the sheriff longer to answer. "Willow and I have been talking," Chris said. "There are three abandoned cabins on the ranch. Two of them are in pretty bad shape, but she says the third one is solid. I think Von might be hiding out there. It's worth checking out."

"Good idea," Travis said. "Where is it?"

"Willow says it's pretty remote—not accessible in a vehicle. We'd need horses. And backup."

"Not something to do in the dark if we don't have to," Travis said. "We'll go in the morning. I'll meet you at five thirty. Does Willow have horses we can use or do I bring my own?" Travis's family owned a large ranch above town.

Chris looked at Willow. "Do you have horses the sheriff can use?"

"Of course."

"See you in the morning," Travis said, and hung up.

"What do we do now?" Willow asked.

He pulled her into his arms and kissed the side of her neck. "We'll just have to find some way to pass the time," he said.

She slid her arms around his neck and arched her body to his. "Maybe we can think of something," she said, and kissed him, long and deep, and he thought that waiting might never be easier.

WILLOW WOKE TO pitch dark and the smell of smoke. She fumbled one hand from beneath the covers and groped on the bedside table for the clock, turning it to face her. Twenty minutes after four in the morning.

She sat up, moving carefully to avoid waking Chris, and tiptoed to the bathroom. When she returned to her room, the smell of smoke hit her again, like wood and burning leaves. The odor penetrated the fog of sleep and sent a stab of fear through her. She hurried to the open window and peered out.

At first, she saw nothing, then a faint glow in the distance drew her attention.

"Chris!" she shouted.

He was out of bed and by her side faster than she would have thought possible. He grasped her arm. "What is it?"

Her throat closed around the horrible words, but she forced them out: "I think the barn is on fire."

Chapter Nineteen

Willow turned and began pulling on clothes, still buttoning her shirt as she ran from the room. She stopped in the kitchen to grab the phone and dial 911, but no one answered. The call didn't even go through. She started to try again, then realized the phone was dead.

Panic swelling to fill her chest and clog her throat, she ran toward the back door, where she shoved her feet into muck boots. She had her hand on the doorknob when Chris jerked her back. "Whoever set the fire and cut the phone lines might be out there," he said.

"I'm not going to let the horses burn," she said, and jerked away from him.

"Go out through the garage," he said. "If someone is watching the house, they might not expect that."

"By 'someone,' you mean Von." She turned toward the garage. "Can you call for help on your radio?" she asked.

He was already keying the microphone. "Dispatch, this is Deputy Chris Delray, reporting a fire in progress at the Russell ranch." He rattled off the address. A woman's voice answered, but it was so distorted by static Willow couldn't make out the words.

"Dispatch, do you copy?" Chris asked.

Another burst of static.

Chris released the mic. "I'll try again in a minute. I need to help you with the horses."

She wanted to race to the barn, to throw open the door and start driving the animals from their stalls, but Chris made her wait. He checked that the coast was clear, then persuaded her she needed to move slowly, sticking to the deepest shadows near outbuildings or trees.

When they reached the barn itself, however, she could hold back no longer. The far end—the section that held equipment and hay, but no animals, was already ablaze. She tried to shove open the big main door, but it refused to budge. Inside, one of the horses whinnied, and another kicked hard at the wall.

Chris helped her wrench open the smaller door on the side of the barn. Willow ran along the center aisle, opening each stall door as she went. Smoke swirled around her, making it difficult to see and more difficult to breathe. "You have to get the main door open!" she shouted over her shoulder.

Chris moved to the main door and shoved hard, but it refused to move, not even when Willow threw her weight behind his. "We'll have to take the horses out through the main door," he said.

She looked down the aisle between the horse stalls. The animals were already panicking, and they would fight going through the narrow entry. But they didn't have a choice. She rushed to the first stall and grabbed the halter of its occupant, Pete, and led him out of the stall. Eyes rolling, clearly frightened, he came with her to the door, where he balked.

"Come on, Pete," she pleaded, and reached to open the door, which had somehow closed behind them. The doorknob turned, but the door itself wouldn't budge. She let go of the horse and threw herself at the door, but it remained fixed.

Then Chris was beside her, adding his strength to hers as they tried to force the door.

"I think it's barricaded from the outside," he said when they had exhausted themselves and leaned, panting, against the door. Smoke stung her eyes and nose and made breathing difficult. By now some of the horses had left their stalls and milled, anxious and whinnying, in the aisle, as the flames popped and crackled behind them.

"We're trapped," she said. Someone—Von King?—had set this fire and barricaded them inside, with no way out.

Chris squinted into the smoke and the mass of milling animals. There had to be another way out. He tried his radio again, but raised nothing but static. His gaze shifted upward. "The loft," he said. "Is there an opening there? We could jump."

Willow nodded, and stumbled toward the ladder to the hayloft. He followed, but before they reached it they saw the whole area was engulfed in flames. The heat, and a choking cloud of smoke, drove them back.

One of the horses began kicking violently at the side of the stall. "They're terrified," Willow said. Tears streaked her face, though Chris couldn't tell if she was crying from her own terror or from the stinging smoke.

"Wet down some horse blankets," he said. The thick wet wool would provide a little protection from the heat and flames, and buy them a few more precious minutes. He went in search of tools, and found a pitchfork and a shovel. He used them to batter at the main door, but it was made of heavy wood and refused to give way. He tried shoving at it with his body, throwing himself at it, but it resisted, as if something heavy blocked it on the other side. He moved down the wall ten feet and began striking there.

Willow joined him, battering at the wood with a shovel. The sound of the fire increased, flames crackling, wood popping, horses screaming and rafters groaning. It was very hard to breathe now, and he fought back panic at the thought of burning to death in here.

Then the wood splintered. Willow cried out and they attacked the weakened boards with more fury, until they gave way. Fresh air rushed to them. He forced his way out and pulled her after him.

Willow stumbled toward the front of the barn. "If we can get the main door open, we can save the horses," she cried.

He spotted the problem as soon as they reached the door—an iron bar wedged in the track the doors needed to slide in. "Willow, wait!" he shouted, intending to tell her he needed to remove the bar first.

A gunshot sounded, loud and distinctive. Willow screamed and dropped to her knees in front of the door.

Chris's vision blurred, even as he dove for cover, automatically reaching for his gun. He blinked to clear his eyes, and forced himself to look, not at Willow's crumpled figure, but in the direction the shots had come from. A shadow moved behind a woodpile opposite the barn.

"Von!" Chris shouted, and fired at the shadow.

"Don't worry, you're next," Von called. He raised a rifle to his shoulder, a weapon with a much greater range than Chris's pistol. Chris fired, anyway, his bullet striking a log in front of Von, sending wood chips flying. It was enough to throw off the other man's aim, the bullet harmlessly hitting the side of the burning barn.

Chris risked a glance at Willow. She lay so still. Too still.

Von raised the rifle again. "Why did you do it?" Chris called. If he could get Von talking, he could buy time. How long before the sheriff was due to arrive at the ranch?

Von lowered the weapon. "Why do you think? For the money."

"The money you thought Sam had hidden?"

"That. And the money Allerton promised me."

So Trey had been right that Von would try to

throw the blame on him. "Allerton promised you money?"

"Money he never paid me. But don't worry, he's next."

"Von, we can talk about this," Chris said.

"I'm done talking."

Willow moaned and both men turned to look at her. She tried to sit up, and her lips moved, but Chris couldn't make out what she was saying. All that mattered was that she was alive.

Von raised his rifle again, aiming not for Chris, but for Willow. Chris stood, deliberately making himself a target. "Von!" he shouted, and when the other man turned his head, Chris fired.

Von dropped the rifle and slumped forward.

"Hold your fire!" someone shouted, and Travis stepped from the shadows in the rocks above and behind Von, a rifle cradled in his arms. "You're a good shot," he said to Chris. "But you didn't have the range with that pistol."

Chris ran to Willow. She tried to stand, but he pushed her back down. Blood ran from a wound in her shoulder. "The horses," she said.

Gage jogged up. "Ambulance and a fire crew are on the way," he said.

Travis joined them. "Get that bar out of the way," he said, indicating the length of metal that was blocking the door. "We have to get these doors open. Chris, get Willow out of the way."

Chris scooped up Willow and carried her away from the barn and the flames. Travis and Gage shoved the doors open and began driving out the horses, shouting and slapping at their rumps, and even prodding at them with the pitchfork to get them to move.

The ambulance arrived, followed by two fire trucks. Others arrived, too—neighbors with horse trailers, and at least one veterinarian, who loaded two animals who had been singed by the blaze and took them away for care.

The ambulance took Willow away and Chris found Travis and Gage among the crowd. "Why did you two show up so early this morning?" he asked.

"Only half an hour early," Gage said. He jerked his thumb toward Travis. "He wanted more time to go over everything before we headed out to arrest Von."

"I'm more than grateful you like to be thorough," Chris said.

Travis nodded, then turned to Gage. "You need to take my weapon," he said, and unfastened his holster. "Chris's, too. As of right now, we're both on mandatory leave while our use of force is investigated. I'm putting you in charge until I'm back on duty."

Gage took their guns. "You'll each need to come by the station and give a statement," he said. "But before then, I need some directions to this cabin where you think Von was hiding. I want to send a couple of deputies up there to collect evidence."

It was late afternoon before Chris made it to the hospital. Willow was out of surgery, awake, but a little groggy. Chris was startled to find his father seated in a chair beside the bed. Ted stood as Chris entered the room. "Willow has been telling me what happened," he said. "Are you all right, son?"

His father's gaze flitted over him, and for the first time Chris realized his hands and clothes were streaked with soot and he reeked of smoke. "I'm okay," he said. "What are you doing here, Dad?"

"I came to give Willow some good news." He looked at her.

Willow nodded. "Tell him."

Ted turned back to Chris. "A judge has ruled Darla's will is invalid. I hired an investigator in Albuquerque who tracked down the witnesses on that document. They both stated they witnessed that will in 2016, not 2019. Darla had carefully changed the date so that it appeared to have been executed after the will I drew up for Sam."

"Your father thinks one of the witnesses called Darla on Tuesday to let her know what was going on and that's the reason she and Emmet left so suddenly," Willow said.

"That is good news." Chris moved to the other side of the bed. "How are you feeling?"

"I'm going to be okay, thanks to you." She squeezed his hand weakly.

Ted stood, as if to leave, but just then a nurse came in. "I need to check the wound, if you would give us a moment, gentlemen," she said.

Ted and Chris moved into the hall. Ted looked at his son as if he had never seen him before. "Willow told me you saved her life," he said. "You killed Von King."

"The sheriff killed Von," Chris said. "I never could have made the shot with my pistol."

"You'd never be faced with something like that working for the state," Ted said.

"Dad…"

"I'm not saying I think that's what you should be doing," Ted said. "I may have believed that before, but I've been thinking a lot about what you said the other night, and about what happened today." He touched Chris's arm. "I don't understand what draws you to this work, but I'm impressed by your dedication. I know you resent the way you think I've tried to run your life, and maybe some of that resentment is justified. When you have children of your own you'll understand this instinct to keep your children safe. So I hope you'll forgive me for my ham-handed attempts to do that."

"I'm not a child for you to protect any longer," Chris said.

"You'll always be my child, but I understand what you're saying. And I didn't raise you to be foolhardy or take unnecessary risks, so there's some comfort in that." He glanced toward the closed door of Willow's hospital room. "Besides, I think now you might have another reason to be careful."

Chris nodded, but said nothing.

"I'll leave you with her," Ted said. "But call if you need anything, okay?"

"Okay, Dad. And…thanks." For helping Willow.

For trying to understand his son's choices. For so much Chris couldn't put into words.

Ted clapped him on the shoulder, then left. The nurse emerged from the room and slipped down the corridor, and Chris went back inside, to the woman who did indeed make him want to be more careful. And more bold.

Epilogue

Two months after she was discharged from the hospital, Willow sat in Ted's office, signing the papers to lease the Double R Ranch to Micah Carstairs, son of her father's former friend Bud. She shook hands with the young rancher once the paperwork was done. "I know you'll do a great job with the place," she said.

Micah nodded. "Thanks for giving me the chance. Dad's excited about seeing the place again. He says it's been too long."

She was still humming with happiness at the rightness of that moment when she met Chris for lunch afterward. "How did it go?" he asked, taking her arm and walking with her toward a booth near the back of the café.

"It went great. I have to think Dad would be pleased. Micah is going to do a much better job with the place than I would have."

"Then I'm happy for you," he said, though she thought his smile didn't reach quite to his eyes.

"Is something wrong?" she asked. "What did you do this morning?"

"The DA had Courtney Baker in for questioning again today," he said. "She stands by her statement that Trey Allerton was with her the morning your father was killed."

"So Von was solely responsible for killing my father."

"We'll never know exactly what happened, but we found one of Von's drinking buddies who confirmed that Von had been talking about getting hold of Sam's hidden riches. After your father fired him, he must have decided to get what he wanted once and for all. We think he took the watch the same way he took the other things he stole—he saw it and wanted it, so he took it. But he threw it away after he realized it would tie him to the crime. Same with the ATV. He took it on impulse, then realized he couldn't keep it. Or maybe he thought ditching it would delay anyone finding Sam's body until he could establish an alibi."

"I hate I lost Dad that way," she said. "But I hope he'd be happy with me leasing the place to Micah. Bud Carstairs and Dad were friends for a long time. It feels good having the families connected again."

He laced his hands with hers. "Can you tell me yet what you've decided to do?"

He had asked her this question only once before. She had told him she had plans, but they weren't firm enough for her to share them. She admired his patience, since she had kept him waiting for weeks. "I'm happy to tell you," she said. She let the silence build, the tension growing, then she laughed. "I'm the new social studies teacher at the high school."

"You're going to teach high school?"

"Yes, and I can't wait. I'm really excited about it."

"It's very different from a full professorship at an eastern university. They didn't mind that you were overqualified?"

"I had to convince them that I didn't see this as a demotion. I'm ready for different. And teaching high school students will be a great challenge for me."

"You'll have to find a new place to live."

"Yes," she said. "And that's going to be a problem. Apparently, there's a shortage of rentals in the area."

He looked down at the table, avoiding her eyes. "I have an idea."

"Oh?"

He shoved out of the booth. "This isn't how I planned to do this," he said.

"To do what?"

He dug into his pocket and pulled out a small box. "I've been carrying this around for a couple of weeks, searching for the right time. I wanted the moment to be special."

"Oh, Chris." She covered both his hands with hers. "It will be special because it's you."

He dropped to one knee beside her. "Willow Russell, will you marry me?"

She was dimly aware of murmurs of conversation around them, and of several people pulling out cell phones to record the moment. She forced her mind away from all of that and stared at the man in beside her. "Oh, Chris."

"Please say yes," he whispered.

"Yes!" She threw her arms around him, then pulled him to his feet. The crowd that had gathered around them broke into applause. He slipped the ring on her finger, then they kissed. "To think when I came home to the ranch, I thought it was the worst thing that could happen," she said. "I never would have believed it could lead to the best."

"You're the best," he said, and kissed her again.

Whatever happened to them now, they would face it together, and look forward to building something completely new.

* * * * *

Look for the next book in Cindi Myers's Eagle Mountain: Search for Suspects miniseries when Missing at Full Moon Mine *goes on sale in March 2022!*

And if you missed the first book in the series, Disappearance at Dakota Ridge, *it's available now wherever Harlequin Intrigue books are sold!*

COMING NEXT MONTH FROM

HARLEQUIN INTRIGUE

#2055 CONARD COUNTY: MISTAKEN IDENTITY

Conard County: The Next Generation • by Rachel Lee

In town to look after her teenage niece, Jasmine Nelson is constantly mistaken for her twin sister, Lily. When threatening letters arrive on Lily's doorstep, ex-soldier and neighbor Adam Ryder immediately steps in to protect Jazz. But will their fragile trust and deepest fears give the stalker a devastating advantage—one impossible to survive?

#2056 HELD HOSTAGE AT WHISKEY GULCH

The Outriders Series • by Elle James

To discover what real life is about, former Delta Force soldier Joseph "Irish" Monahan left the army and didn't plan to need his military skills ever again. But when a masked stalker attempts to murder Tessa Bolton, Irish is assigned as her bodyguard and won't abandon his mission to catch the killer *and* keep Tessa alive.

#2057 SERIAL SLAYER COLD CASE

A Tennessee Cold Case Story • by Lena Diaz

Still haunted by the serial killer she couldn't catch, police detective Bree Clark doesn't hesitate to accept PI Ryland Beck's offer of redemption. The Smoky Mountain Slayer cold case has gone hot again and working together could bring the murderer to justice. But is the culprit the original slayer—or a dangerous copycat?

#2058 MISSING AT FULL MOON MINE

Eagle Mountain: Search for Suspects • by Cindi Myers

Deputy Wes Landry knows he shouldn't get emotionally involved with his assignments. But a missing person case draws him to Rebecca Whitlow. Desperate to find her nephew, she's worried the rock climber has gotten lost...or worse. Something dangerous is happening at Full Moon Mine—and they're about to get caught in the thick of it.

#2059 DEAD GIVEAWAY

Defenders of Battle Mountain • by Nichole Severn

Deputy Easton Ford left Battle Mountain—and the woman who broke his heart—behind for good. Now his ex-fiancée, District Attorney Genevieve Alexander, is targeted by a killer, and he's the only man she trusts to protect her. But will his past secrets get them both killed?

#2060 MUSTANG CREEK MANHUNT

by Janice Kay Johnson

When his ex, Melinda McIntosh, is targeted by a paroled criminal, Sheriff Boyd Chaney refuses to let the stubborn officer be next on the murderer's revenge list. Officers and their loved ones are being murdered and the danger is closing in. But will their resurrected partnership be enough to keep them safe?

Still haunted by the serial killer she couldn't catch, police detective Bree Clark doesn't hesitate to accept PI Ryland Beck's offer of redemption. The Smoky Mountain Slayer cold case has gone hot again and working together could bring the murderer to justice. But is the culprit the original slayer—or a dangerous copycat?

Read on for a sneak preview of Serial Slayer Cold Case, *part of A Tennessee Cold Case Story series, from Lena Diaz.*

Chapter One

Maintaining a white-knuckle grip on the steering wheel while negotiating the treacherous curves up Prescott Mountain on his daily commute was typical for Ryland Beck. *Smiling* while he resolutely refused to look toward the steep drop on the other side of the road *wasn't* typical. Nothing, not even his phobia of heights, could dampen his enthusiasm this chilly October morning. Today he'd begin his investigation into a serial killer case that had gone cold over four years ago.

Bringing down the Smoky Mountain Slayer was the challenge of a lifetime. No suspects. No DNA. No viable behavioral profile. In spite of the lack of evidence, Ryland was determined to put the killer behind bars. He wanted to give the families of the five victims the answers and justice they deserved.

Unfortunately, what he couldn't give them was closure. Closure, as he well knew, was a fictional construct. The death of a loved one would always leave a gaping hole in the hearts and lives of those left behind. But knowing the victim's murderer had been caught and punished would go a long way toward making the excruciating grief more bearable.

He continued winding his way up the mountain toward UB headquarters as he considered the limited information he'd found on the internet about the killings. The Slayer's modus operandi was consistent: all of his victims were strangled, their bodies dumped in the woods in Monroe County. But aside from them being young women, the victimology was all over the place. Their educational and economic backgrounds varied, as did their ethnicity. Some were married, some weren't. Some had children, some didn't. All of that made it nearly impossible to build a useful profile to help figure out who'd murdered them.

The detectives from the Monroe County Sheriff's Office had deemed the case unsolvable. But here in Gatlinburg, Ryland had a unique advantage: an über-wealthy boss who knew firsthand the suffering a victim's family endured when a murder case went cold.

Seven years after his wife was killed and his infant daughter went missing, Grayson Prescott had given up on the stagnant police investigation. He decided to create a cold case company called Unfinished Business. Just a few months later, UB had solved the case. Now, the thirty-three counties of the East Tennessee region had formed a partnership with UB and were clamoring for them to work their cold cases.

HIEXP0122B